W. B. Shoemaker

Florida as It Is

It tells all about the industries of the state, its climate and resources

W. B. Shoemaker

Florida as It Is
It tells all about the industries of the state, its climate and resources

ISBN/EAN: 9783337369552

Printed in Europe, USA, Canada, Australia, Japan

Cover: Foto ©Andreas Hilbeck / pixelio.de

More available books at **www.hansebooks.com**

FLORIDA AS IT IS

IT TELLS ALL ABOUT THE INDUS-
TRIES OF THE STATE, ITS CLI-
MATE AND RESOURCES.

*Written in Common Sense Language without
paint or varnish,*

/BY

DR. W. B. SHOEMAKER.

1887.

NEWVILLE, PA., TIMES STEAM PRINT.

INTRODUCTION.

Be it known to all the world and the rest of mankind, that within the last few years, much has been said and written about Florida, extolling this land of "Sunshine and Flowers. Many, if not all of these descriptions have some truth in them, but much of it is so embellished, in such glowing colors and only the bright side shown, that many persons come to the conclusion at once that if they can only get to this land of promise (by those interested) that sickness and sorrow will never reach them and that labor and trouble will vex them never more.

This little book has been written with a view to undeceive such persons; to take the glamor from these stories and to show "Florida as it is" without paint or varnish, that is the good and bad that has to be encountered in this land, to show people what they must do here and how to do it.

I do not propose to write a history or geography of the State, but simply to state the facts as they would present themselves to you were you to take a trip through the State at this time.

I will describe the manner of living, the state of society, the cultivation of the soil, (sand) clearing lands, draining marshes, planting and cultivating orange groves, tropical fruits, the kind of houses the people live in, the kind and quality of stock they raise, the game and fish they have, the mosquitos and pests that are there—in fact I propose that this little book, "Florida As It Is" shall be to the reader a complete trip all over Florida at a very small cost; that the same information in the usual way of traveling would cost you hundreds of dollars and then you would have no more accurate information and no more of it than you will have after a careful reading of this book. I have also aimed to write the book in plain common sense language so that any and every person can, and will understand it. I have tried to avoid all personalities so as to give offense to none.

I have given the facts as they are without fear or favor. I have had very little outside aid. The entire book is my own observation and experience. being right on the ground and I will only say, that after reading the book you will know more about Florida, its ins and outs and pros and cons, than nine-tenths of the people who have spent a season there and in addition saved much money.

THE AUTHOR.

FLORIDA AS IT IS.

Florida was discovered by Juan Ponce de Leon, April 4th, 1512. In 1539 it was explored and in 1565 a body of French Calvinists, who had established a settlement three years previous, were driven out by the Spaniards—the latter held possession until 1763, when it reverted to England by session in 1781. The Spaniards regained possession of the country and two years later were confirmed in their possession by the peace of Versailles. In 1820 Florida was ceded by Spain to the United States, received a territorial constitution in 1833, and was admitted into the Union as a State, March 3d, 1845.

Florida is located in the extreme Southern part of the United States, between latitudes 24 and 31, and longitude 80 and 88 West from Greenwich. Its greatest length North and South is about 500 miles, and the longest line from East to West is about 400 miles. The State is amorphous in shape being neither round, oval, oblong or square. Its area is about 60,000 square miles or about the size of Pennsylvania, New Jersey, Delaware, Connecticut and Rhode Island all put together.

The State is bounded on the North by Georgia and Alabama, on the west by Alabama and the Gulf of Mexico, on the South by the Gulf of Mexico and on the east by the Atlantic Ocean.

The State is divided into forty counties, and the area or surface of the State is land and water. The land may be divided or classed as follows :

High Pine, Flat Woods Pine, Scrub Pine, Gray or Rolling Hammock, Low Hammock, Cypress, Marsh and Swamp Lands.

The water may be and is divided into lakes, rivers, creeks, springs, ponds and bay heads.

LAKES.

There are thousands of lakes in the State, ranging in size from less than a quarter of an acre to thousands of acres in extent. Lake Ocheechobee alone, covers not less than half a million of acres of land.

Lake Apopka covers not less than forty thousand acres East and West; Tohopekaligas about the same. There are very many other lakes that cover from ten to ten thousand acres, and some of them much more. Most of these lakes are very deep and the water in them is clear and said to be pure in nearly all of them. A great many of these

lakes, especially the smaller ones have nice sloping banks, which, with the bottoms are sandy, and
perfectly safe to enter. or drive into the lakes in so
far as swamping is concerned. but it is always well
enough to go slowly when in the water, or you
may get beyond your depth before you are aware
of it; many persons have lost their lives by ventur-
ing too far in places of this kind.

Some of the larger, and a few of the smaller
lakes and ponds have quick-sand holes. These
are specially to be avoided, for should you by ac-
cident or otherwise, get into one of these holes or
places, your chances for getting out would be very
slim indeed, unless help was right at hand. Some
of these lakes, both large and small, have what
they call muck bottoms. This muck is nothing
more or less than the accumulation of decayed
vegetable matter that has been accumulating for
ages; these when drained make the richest and
best vegetable and sugar-cane land in the State
and perhaps in the world, and here is where the
Disston Land and Drainage Company are making
their money.

RIVERS.

There are quite a number of rivers (so called)
in the State, the largest of which is the St. Johns.
The peculiarity of this river is that it flows Northward, while the entire State seems to fall off
toward the South, and eventually sinks into the

Gulf of Mexico. Notwithstanding all this, the
current of this river is toward the North. This
river is navigable for more than two hundred miles,
and a very large class of steamers ply on it from
Jacksonville to Sanford, a distance of about two
hundred miles and make regular daily trips.
Smaller steamers run beyond Sanford, it being the
head of navigation for large steamers before the
era of railroads in Florida. The St. Johns was
about the only highway on which travel was had,
and merchandise could be shipped from the sea-
board to the interior of the State. Some of the
other rivers of note are Suwanee, Appalachicola,
Oklockonee. Ancilla, Santa Fee, Withlacoochee,
Pease, Caloosahatchee, Kissimmee, Ocklawaha,
Indian and Wekiva. The most of these rivers or
waters are navigable for small steamers and are
thus utilized. There are other rivers or rather
kind of natural canals leading from one lake to
another. Many of these are being dredged and
cleaned out so that small steam boats can run cut
of one lake into another, thus in many cases, making water navigation from place to place for remember that very many of the larger lakes have
steamers on them, both for freight traffic and
pleasure. Nearly all streams that have any current at all are called rivers. The streams in
Florida are nearly all sluggish, as for example
the St. Johns River is said to have only a fall of

six feet in two hundred miles, and were you to
travel on it you would probably say it had no current at all. It is very crooked; some of the bends
being so short that the larger steamers sometimes
have difficulty in getting through. I know of no
streams of any length in the State that have a current of more than a mile in a half day. There are
also many waters here called rivers, that are nothing more or less than arms of the Gulf or Atlantic,
extending inland as the Indian River. This river
is on the east coast and separated from the Atlan-
ic, by a strip of land, very narrow in places and
wider in other places. This water has no current,
its surface being on a level with the Atlantic Ocean.
Said by some persons to be two feet higher than
the Atlantic Ocean.

UNDERGROUND RIVERS AND SPRINGS.

There seems to be and certainly is, underground
rivers here as is proven by such large streams
bursting out of the ground as Silver Springs.
This spring covers about four acres of ground and
is from forty to sixty feet deep, and the run from
it is one of the principal sources of the Ocklawaha
River and good sized steamers come up the run
into the springs

Clay Springs is another of the same kind, only
not quite so large. Glen Cove, Funiak and many
others demonstrate the fact that there are many
underground streams in Florida.

Again streams of water and even lakes suddenly

disappear. Lake Levy, a body of water which, when full, covers about twelve hundred acres, has been totally dry, the water disappearing in a few days, and in one instance remaining so for several years and nearly all the bottom was farmed in corn and cotton. There was only a small river running where the lake was and it disappeared about where the centre of the lake was. This hole seemed to fill up and the ground became covered with water again.

This has occurred several times within the last fifty years. The lake is now full of water and is known as Lake Levy or Paines Prairie. No person knows how soon or when the bottom of the lake will again fall out.

Between Orange Lake and Micanopy, as well as in the neighborhood of Gainesville, there are great holes in the earth. The bottom is far below the surface of the lakes in the surrounding country. Some of these holes or sinks are more than one hundred feet deep, and several hundred feet in diameter at the top, and are funnel shaped. Many of them are perfectly dry, and have large trees growing inside nearly to the bottom. The tops of many of them does not reach as high as the surface of the ground surrounding the hole.

Others of these holes are barren of trees and there is water at the bottom. How deep this water is, I had no means of finding out and no person could tell me anything about it. The fact is, the natives seem to be afraid of these places and do not care to go near them. There is not even any signs that cattle or stock of any kinds goes near the holes, especially those that have water in them.

There are some natural curiosities in Florida, and they are of such a nature that I know of nowhere else in the world that the same kind exist. Take for instance this Silver Spring, which is a veritable Niagara Falls, turned upside down, and if the reader should ever visit Florida, do not fail to see it, with its pure, clear pellucid waters, big cat fish and other kinds of fish, and where you can drop a nickel or any other small coin or substance and watch its descent until it strikes the bottom from forty to sixty feet below you. The water is so clear that you can see objects on the bottom about as plainly as if there was no water there at all.

PONDS AND CREEKS.

Ponds are grass lakes, usually with mud or muck bottoms, and are inhabited with frogs, alligators and other things too numerous to mention. Creeks are connections between sloughs or cypress swamps, as Shingle Creek, near Kissimmee, or Sweet Water Creek, near Bayard, in Duval county and many others.

FISH AND OYSTERS.

In nearly all of the waters of Florida there are abundance of Fish, Trout, (Black Bass), Strawberry Bass (Perch,) Blue and Mud Catfish, some of which are very large. They say there are other fish here also, such as Bream, Red Horse, White Fish, Eels. &c. This may be, but I have seen none of the latter.

There are a great many oysters, both on the Gulf and Atlantic Coasts of Florida, but they are very small and inferior in every way, to the oysters farther North-East; there is no care taken of these oyster beds, and it is said many of them are being destroyed by wash from rivers and streams, covering them up with sand and other debris. These are called Coon Oysters, and certainly would not be relished by the epicure or conconnoisseur.

ALLIGATORS.

There are thousands and millions of Alligators of all sizes from a few inches in length to almost fifteen or more feet. There seems to be but one species of alligators, and all the difference there is in them is in size alone. They can, and do live both in and out of the water. They are not dangerous except when wounded on their nests or hibernating grounds are molested. A ten feet alligator can crush a man's body with his jaws or kill him with a strike of his tail.

At mating time frequent fights occur between the males At such times you can hear them hollow for miles. Their hollowing is something like a mad bull.

They are a heavy, ugly and ungainly animal,

and are something after the shape of an enormous Lizzard. They are web footed and their hind legs are much longer than their front ones, and are attached higher up or nearer the back than the front ones and their legs are unproportionately close together. They swim slowly in the water—more like floating than otherwise, and when swimming or floating. their bodies are about one-third out of the water.

Their movements on land are usually slow and awkward, but when pursued or pursuing, they can, and do travel as fast, or faster than a man can walk, or even run for a short distance. They move on land in very nearly a straight line. They are so formed that that they cannot make short turns or curves when in motion on land. Notwithstanding all this, you should not fool with them when at rest, as they sometimes make very awkward motions with their tails and jaws, and you cannot always tell what kind of a move they may make. There is some danger of being bitten or receiving a stroke with their tail.

Their traveling on land is principally in the night time or on dark cloudy days during a rain or immediately after a shower, when they frequently go from one lake or swamp to another. On fair. warm and sunshiny days you can see thousands of them basking on old logs and stumps on the banks of the lakes something after the style of little turtles in the mill-dams of the North.

Their nests or hibernating grounds are formed by themselves. where the water is rather shallow or on a knoll or kind of island   They collect all manner of stuff, pieces of logs, sticks, brush, grass. moss, pine knots and indeed nothing seems to come amiss to them.   This is all formed into a mass with mud, muck and wild cabbage leaves and sand. These nests when completed, rise several feet above the surface of the water and are kind of saucer shaped or scooped out on the top.   Here they deposit their eggs, and cover them, and nature does the balance

The "gators" however do not leave this locality during incubation, and here let me say it is rather dangerous to examine these nests. or even approach them unless you are well armed and have a steady nerve and well prepared to do battle. for unless somebody has been there before you and killed the "gators," you are sure to see them and they will be upon you before you are aware if not on your guard, and sometimes as many as a dozen will approach you from different points and here they are dangerous.   If however you have a good Winchester or some other good repeating rifle of about forty-four calibre and are a good and true shot, you need not have much to fear, for if you kill one or two of them, the others will soon disappear, and here let me say, the fatal spot to hit an Alligator is right in the lower part of the neck or right behind the front leg, below the middle.   You can sometimes kill them by shooting them in the eye or through the body, but it is not a sure thing

The mouth of the "gator" contains eighty-four teeth. Forty in the lower and forty-four in the upper jaws, and they are all canine or sharp pointed, and some of them in a big "gator" are as much as three inches long, and are very irregular, and if one becomes broken nature replaces it.

The head of a ten foot "gator" is just about the size of an ordinary horse head. The jaws are full length of the head. The condyles or hinges are on the neck, so you see when he opens his mouth the entire head is in two pieces AS IT WERE. Imagine a horse to be able open his mouth clear up to his ears and you can have an idea of a "gator's" mouth. It is no trouble for a "gator" to swallow a good chunk or a dog or a little nigger at one swallow, both of which it is said, they are very fond of.

The top or upper part of the head is very flat and the bones are from a half to three-quarters of an inch thick, hence you might about as well shoot against a rock as against a "gator's" head to kill him. They feed on just about anything that comes in their way. In many instances pine knots have been found in their stomachs, worn as smooth as glass.

DISSTON LAND AND DRAINAGE COMPANY.

The head quarters of the company is at Kissimmee City, a town of three or four years growth, situated on the North shore of West Tohopekaliga. The city now is said to have about twelve hundred inhabitants. I think however if eight hundred were taken out of the town, but few would be left. This Disston Company was formed three or four years ago. They built several steam and dredge boats, and went to work to lower the lakes of East and West Tohopekaliga by opening a canal through a kind of natural drain or water way into Lake Ocheechobee. After their engineer corps had surveyed and gone over the route, their report seemed to show that there was a fall of some seventy feet from the south end of Lake Tohopekaliga to Punta Rassa on the Gulf Coast, and that Tohopekaliga through the natural channel had a fall of about one inch to the mile, which, by proper canalling, &c., could be increased by shortening the distance to at least three inches to the mile, which would, by their calculation, drain and reclaim about five million acres of land. An arrangement was made with the State that the company should have half of all the land in fee simple that should be thus reclaimed. On these conditions the company went to work, commencing at the South end of Tohopekaliga and cut a canal some three or four miles into Cypress Lake, and from thence into Lake Kissimmee five or six miles. This canal is wide and deep enough to allow a good sized steamboat to pass through. It was found as soon as the canal was opened, that the water in Tohopekaliga would be drawn off to a certain extent, though these canals are carried into Ocheechobee through the Kissimmee River.

The next move was to cut a canal. a distance of about three miles, thereby connecting East and West Tohopekaliga Lakes; this was accomplished. Then the Kissimmee River was next cleaned out, dredged and shortened, thus opening a water navigation for steamers and other boats into Lake Ocheechobee. This lake seems to have no natural outlet, but near the South end of it and about four miles westward, is Lake Hickpochee, which is the head water of the Caloosahatchee River. To work, the company went and cut a canal from Ocheechobee into this lake and then opened and dredged the last named river, which runs through Lake Flirt, and thus completed the water route to Punta Rassa on San Carlos Bay on the Gulf of Mexico. This, however did not seem to lower the water in Ocheechobee very much. They are now trying to drain this latter lake into the St. Lucie Sound on the Atlantic coast, thus necessitating the cutting of a canal through swamps and other lands, a distance of some thirty miles. A part of this work is done, but it will be sometime before it is completed. And what effect it will have when completed is yet to be determined. One thing however is a fixed fact, the company have opened water communication from Kissimmee City to the

Gulf, and steamers and sail boats are making trips between these points and they have lowered the waters in both the Tohopekaliga Lakes, about five feet thus reclaiming. The company claims about two and a half million acres. I think the claims are too large, but be this as it may, there are thousands of acres of as good land as there is in Florida under cultivation to-day that was two years ago covered with water, and thousands of acres more are being prepared to plant sugar cane and vegetables. Should this company fail to re-claim any more land, they have already done a grand work, both for the State and themselves.

HIGH PINE LANDS.

Now the reader must not understand that any of the lands in Florida are very much elevated above the level of the ocean or large lakes. Take the State throughout and it is flat—very flat, more so than in Kansas, but still there are elevations and depressions, none of which exceed a very few hundred feet. I suppose the elevations about cor-respond with the depressions.

The term "High Pine Lands," as well as the other descriptive terms used, are relative terms and used more to designate the kind and quality of the land than its elevation, "High Pine" Land would be just as well designated, and perhaps better by calling it dry pine land, and that is just what it is. This land is among the highest in the State The best quality of this land is covered with a growth ol large yellow pine trees. some of which are curly pine, and very valuable. The trees are nearly all large, some ol them as much as two and a half and three feet across the stump and from fifty to seventy-five feet without a limb. When sawed into timber, it is worth from thirteen to twenty-two dollars per thousand feet at the mill, and the curly pine is worth trom forty to fifty dollars per thousand when sawed into lumber at the mill This kind of land you will usually find in the neighborhood of deep lakes with sand bottoms and rather high, sloping banks—the trees growing nearly to the water's edge.

Occasionally in the high pine lands, you will find here and there a scrubby live oak. The undergrowth is wild oats. This is a kind of rough grass that grows tall and not at all thickly on the ground. It is not good for much. Stock will eat it when they can get nothing else.

There is very little Bramble or Palmetto on this kind of land, hence it is easily cleared and prepared for cultivation and when it is well fertilized will produce melons, beans, cucumbers, corn, and sweet potatoes, and makes excellent orange land. Many prefer this kind of land for oranges and all the semi-tropical fruits; particularly those of the citrus family, for the reason that it costs less to clean up and prepare for a crop. The timber, if at all within the reach of a mill, will much more than pay for the clearing and planting of a grove, while the cost of clearing Hammock lands will more than pay for fertilizer to bring a grove into bearing.

Again orange trees on high pine land are not subject to "Die Back" or foot rot. This disease is said to be caused by the tap root of the trees striking the water or hard pan, which they are almost certain to do in low lands. The soil, if soil it may be called, is nearly all pure sand—white on top—after removing the top, it is of a yellowish color, and the yellower the sand is the better the land is said to be.

SCRUB PINE OR BLACK JACK LAND.

This kind of land is partially covered with scrubby pines, a kind of dwarf oak called Black Jack, a few scraggy, little live oaks and kind of thorny, rough bramble. This kind of land in my judgement, is of such a nature that it never can be utilized for anything. The soil is white sand from top to bottom, and I guess the more a man owned the poorer he would be.

LOW OR FLAT WOODS PINE LAND.

This is called second class pine land. It has a good deal of pine timber on it, also Live Oak and sometimes a little Water Oak, not usually heavy timbered, and the timber is not of as good quality as that on the high pine land. It has much more white or sap wood than the other or high pine. It does not grow so large as the other

and it is a rarity to see a curly pine on this kind of
land. This has an undergrowth of scrub. (Hog)
and saw Palmetto, sometimes of pretty dense
growth and is hard to clear and grub and when it
is prepared for cultivation is pretty good for vegetables, grapes, guavas and strawberries. It is
very poor land for oranges, or indeed any of the
citrus family. It will do for pine apples and bananas. The soil is a blackish mold, (from decayed)
vegetation,) for half an inch or so on top, then
white sand for ten to fifteen or more inches, when
you get to a kind of brownish quick sand that is
usually from a few inches to several feet in thickness. Under this is a kind of a hard pan which
seems to separate or divide the surface water from
that below. This hard pan seems to be formed of
very fine, grayish sand, and is almost impervious
to water and very hard and usually about a foot
thick. To get water at all fit to drink, you must
go below this stratum.

Remember to raise crops on this land, you must
fertilize and that heavily and constantly. We may
as well say it here as elsewhere that fertilizing is
the key note to all the vegetables and fruits raised
in Florida with perhaps one exception, and that is
sweet potatoes and a little of it does not hurt them
by any means.

HAMMOCK LANDS.

Are of two kinds, rolling or high and flat or low
Hammock. This word Hammock seems to be pe-

culiar to Florida. The word originally meant a
solid mass of turf, considerably elevated above the
surrounding earth, then spelled Hommock, or
Hummock, then the Indians called any little
hillock, or small eminence of a rather conical form,
whether covered with trees or not, a Hommock,
but now the people of Florida call any piece of land
whether high or low, that produces hard-wood
trees, such as oak, hickory, ash, magnolia, &c.,
Hammock lands and the original Hammock is now
called reclaimed marsh land. This will enable the
reader to fairly or properly understand what is
meant by Hammock lands. All land on which
hard wood predominate, whether high or low, are
called Hammock land, and all lands on which pine
predominates, are called pine lands.

ROLLING OR GRAY HAMMOCK

Land is usually covered with a heavy growth of
timber, such as oak, hickory, magnolia and all the
hard woods that grow in the State. The undergrowth of palmetto, green briars, devils staff, (a
kind of prickly ash) and other bramble is very hard
to clear and get in shape for cultivation, and costs
a great amount of outlay, but when once got into
shape, produces well and with fertilizer can be
made to produce immense crops of vegetables and
strawberries. This is also the best of orange land
provided it is high enough above the water level.

FLAT HAMMOCKS

Are much lower than the other kind, and have a

much denser growth both timber, and undergrowth
than the former, consequently are much harder to
clear off and prepare for cultivation. but when
brought under cultivation are among the best lands
in the State, and if any land in the State will produce crops without being fertilized,this kind of
land will. and this produces much better by being
fertilized.   On this land you can raise vegetables
of all kinds that will grow here, provided the bugs.
VARMINTS, and insects let them alone.   In abundance you can also raise lemons. grapes, guavas.
pine apples, bananas. and many other of the semi-
tropical fruits and berries.

Orange trees, as a general thing. do not do well
on flat hammock, except where wild orange stocks
are used, which can be, and are frequently budded
with sweet orange buds and do well.

The famous "Bishop and Harris" Grove on
Orange Lake in Levy County, was started in this
way, than which there is none better in the State.
but this is the exception rather than the rule.

SWAMP LANDS.

These are almost useless and are not susceptible
of reclamation, being very low and thickly set with
cypress trees and other water plants, vines and
trees.   There is thousands of acres in some of these
swamps. into which the foot of man has never trod.
and never will. or if he attempts it, the chances of
his ever again getting out are all against him.   Enormous alligators, venemous snakes, reptiles.

poisonous insects and dangerous wild animals are
there.

Many of these swamps are trackless, pathless—
wilderness in every sense of the word, as for example the Big Cypress Swamp in Monroe county,
which covers not less than seven hundred thous-
and acres of territory in nearly a solid body. This,
however is the largest cypress swamp in the State.
There are, however, thousands of cypress and
other swamps in the State that cover from one to
ten thousand and more acres each, and many of
them just as impenetrable as the Big Cypress
Swamp.

THE CYPRESS TREE

Has some peculiarities that seem to entitle it to a
particular description. It seems to stand alone
among the trees, particularly in that. It is always
found in clusters and very few, if any other trees
will grow, or do grow where the cypress has once
taken hold. Sometimes you will find a few cabbage, palmettos and it may be a scraggy live oak
in the edge of a cypress clump or swamp. The
tree seems to belong to the fir or pine family in that
its leaves or foliage is of that nature. It is neither
a deciduous nor yet an evergreen, yet its foliage
is green almost the entire year. It pushes out new
foliage each year and the old one remains on until
the new starts. So the tree presents the appearance of being clipped (so to say) once a year.

These trees all grow or have their roots in the water, and the peculiarity of their formation is that their roots or knees, as they are called here, are very much the larger part of them. The tap, or main root is said to be as far under the water as the top extends above it. The base of the tree for the first eight or ten feet after it leaves the water, is cone shaped, then it grows up straight and presents a beautiful appearance, having but few limbs or boughs and putting on a nice umbrella shaped top.

These trees usually grow from fifty to a hundred feet in height. A cypress tree that is one foot in diameter, ten feet from the surface of the water, is perhaps from six to ten feet in diameter at the surface of the water. The roots or knees seem to widen out, locking and interlocking and overlapping each other, thus forming a complete net work of the biggest kind of stumps and roots, covering acres and acres, and in many cases miles and miles of territory.

The trees may be cut off. They make good lumber, shingles and posts. The stumps and roots remain and as time seems to have no effect on them so far as decay is concerned, they still remain and become almost as hard as iron, hence the utter impossibility of utilizing these swamps, even if they could be drained, which is, as a general thing about as impossible as to get rid of the stumps and roots, there being no place into which they can be drained.

These swamps are well defined and are usually found in the pine regions. Hardly ever find a Cypress swamp and Hammock land adjoining. They do not seem to have any affinity for each other.

A beautiful sight is a Cypress swamp. The green foliage of the trees all covered with gray moss, and it hanging from the limbs of the trees in long festoons, and they waving in the breeze and the sparkling water underneath, and the mosquitos buzzing, the alligators bellowing, tne frogs croaking and the parokeets chattering. It is a sight and scene once seen and heard will never be forgotten.

THE COUNTRY AT LARGE.

The general appearance of the country is rather flat. It is flat, and to the eyes of a Northern man or Northern people, presents rather a sorry and desolate appearance. (I now speak of the country away from the towns and cities), and about the first question that is asked is. "what do you do or what can you raise here to make a living, and what have you to back up your country?" and about a hundred more of the same sort.

We see no grass, no grain of any kind growing. The groves we pass seem to be set in nothing but pure sand, and that of the sandiest kind; not even a stone or rock of any kind to vary the monotony. The road we are travelling on is nothing but sand,

and that from a few inches to a foot deep.
The horses step in the loose sand every step to
their pasterns, and the wheels of the carriage sink
into the sand about as deeply as do the horses feet
If you drive faster than the walk, the wheels carry
the sand around and soon your clothes, shoes and
the carriage are full of sand, and when you arrive
at your journey's end and examine yourself, you
will find that you are pretty well covered with sand
yourself. About now you will begin to find out
that there is something besides sand in the soil, for
instead of shaking and brushing it off, you will
find that it takes soap, water and labor, or rubbing
to get the stuff off you, especially off your body.
This substance, which is mixed with sand along
with fertilizer and climate, makes the soil productive. The soil on top looks very much alike in
the pine lands—simply white sand on top for a few
inches, then it becomes of a yellowish color, except in the scrub pine or black jack lands, where
the sand is white, I reckon to the bottom.

In the Hammocks, the sand is of a dark color on
the top for several inches and sometimes for several feet, then usually quick sand underneath except
in the lower Hammocks, which are usually covered
for several inches on top with vegetable mold. In
some places this vegetable mold is several feet
thick; under this is sand. In all the low lands at
a certain depth from the surface—some places
deeper than others, is a kind of dividing line or

hard pan that seems to divide the water. That
above is brackish and not fit for use unless it be
first boiled and strained, but when you penetrate
or dig through this hard pan, and either pipe or
curb out the wild or surface water, you obtain
water that can be drank and used for cooking purpose and those persons who like it, say it is good
and wholesome—to me it is warm and tasteless.

The water business in more senses than one, is
the worst drawback Florida has to contend with.
The soil is of such a nature that brick or cemented
cisterns in the ground are nearly an impossibility.
The only remedy is to have large tanks made of
Cypress wood and catch rain water, then if you
are where ice can be had, you can manage to get
along, provided you can keep the wiggletails cut
of your tank.

THE EVERGLADES.

There is a vast scope of country lying in the Southern part of the State, principally in Monroe and
Dade counties. It is a kind of marsh—the most of
it is covered with water. It is a kind of net work
of rivers lakes and ponds, lagoons and bay heads
where the ground rises above the water. It produces the rankest kind of tropical and semi-tropical vegetation, cane brakes and saw grass of immense growth are there, and were you to become
lost in the brakes or entangled in the saw grass,
you would in all probability die right there. The

most of Florida's cultivated fruits grow there in a wild state. The Mango or Mangrove grows wild and can be eat, though not very palatable. The land seems to be highest along the coast and some few people live down there and eke out an existence by hunting, fishing, trying to cultivate the cocoanut and tame the Mangrove.

The Disston Land and Drainage Company are working on the North end of the Glades and they think if they can succeed in draining Ocheechobee Lake and lowering the water from six to ten feet that quite a large portion of the Everglades can be cultivated. This, no doubt would be the case, could the drainage be made. The bottoms of the lakes, rivers, ponds. &c., of the Glades are composed of decayed vegetable matter that has been accumulating for thousands of years, but in my judgment a company that should undertake to enlarge the borders of the State of New Jersey by undertaking to drain the Atlantic Ocean, would be about as successful as this company will be in draining the Everglades of Florida.

MARSH LAND.

These are sometimes called swamp lands, but there is about the same difference between Cypress swamps and Marsh land as there is between the poorest Scrub Pine land and the richest Hammocks The Marshes are a kind of low prairie or shallow bay head, extending or running out from the lakes in the low country. They are partly covered with water during the greater part of the year and wholly covered in a wet time. They receive and retain all the wash from the higher lands, and there is always a rank growth of vegetable matter on and surrounding them, which decays and thus enriches them. This growth and decay has been going on for ages, until now there is many feet deep of this deposited in them.

This is the kind of land that first attracted the attention of the Disston Land and Drainage Company.

When these Marshes are drained and brought under cultivation, they are among the very best lands in the State, if not in the world for raising sugar cane and all kinds of vegetables, and it is said that Irish potatoes do very well if planted in January or February on these lands. Thousands and thousands of acres of these Marshes have been reclaimed within the last three years, on which there is now growing sugar cane, cabbage and all kinds of vegetables that can be grown in this climate.

In some cases orange trees have been planted on land thus reclaimed, and so far they seem to grow and do well. How they will do when the tap root reaches the water level is yet to be seen. Any and all trees that have no tap root, such as lemon, guava, peach, &c., do well on reclaimed Marsh land. Bananas do first rate, but pine apples not so well as they require a sandy soil. The beauty of these lands are that they, and they alone will produce crops for an indefinite length of time without fertilizer, and indeed, this reclaimed Marsh land when hauled out and spread on pine land, acts as a fertilizer itself. As before stated, many thousands of acres of this kind of land have been reclaimed, and there is yet thousands of acres of the same kind of land in the State that can, and no doubt will be reclaimed in the near future.

SEASONS AND CLIMATE,

Both are rather peculiar in this peninsula. The seasons, so to speak are only two, winter and summer. The winters are short, and in the South half of Florida, snow has never been seen; no, not by the oldest inhabitant, and seldom any severe frosts, but I do not know that I can give any description that will fill the bill better than to quote from a letter recently published in the *Weekly Times*.

"Some one has said take the climate from Florida and the State will be the very poorest of them all. That would be the exact truth except for one impossible fact If the present climate of Florida were taken away, it would of necessity have another climate, because no place on the globe can exist climateless. Therefore, to take away the climate of Florida would be the same as to give it another climate and that climate might be worse, or it might be better. To give to Florida the climate of Denmark, Morocco or Mexico, would give it a worse one than we now have, but to give it the climate of South Japan, Hawaii or San Domingo would be a slight improvement upon the liabilities to frosts from the cold waves of winter, but neu for the balance of the year.

Climate is as much a part of any country as its soil, and until there shall be a....u.e change of the climatical conditions of the atmosphere, the climate peculiar to each region must remain as at present. Such changes have taken place during the first periods that have existed since the most ancient rocks were first formed and they may occur again. Florida may become as it was. When tropical heats produce the immense vegetable growths of the carbonaceous period or in later periods when the elephant, rhinocerous and tapir fed on the plains at the head of the Mississippi and the Mastoden and Megatherium browsed the tropical herbage of Florida, so may Florida again have the climate that existed when the whole of the Northern States were covered with ice and snow a thousand feet deep and those regions had glaciers and climate conditions now presented in the Northern Greenland.

The man who buys a farm in Florida, buys the climate as well as the soil and the plants upon it ; the atmosphere above the mineral below the surface become his The acres of climate corresponds to the acres of the surface. Florida without its climate would not be Florida. It would be shorn of its best qualities or would be improved, who can tell which.

This matter of the climate of Florida should never be lost sight of in considering questions pertaining to the healthfulness and capabilities of the State, especially should the person who plants a crop raise an animal, writes, talks about or gives advice concerning agricultural subjects, bear constantly in mind that Florida has a climate, ·"Sui Generis" (particularly to its own) that must remain with all the equability consistent with the geographical situation. It must not be lost sight of for a moment that each December and January a frost more or less severe will occur in all the Northern half of the State. That between the summer solstice and the autumnal Equinox, is the season of greatest rains, cooling showers and greatest humidity of the atmosphere and the period of greatest vegetable growth ; that May and early June is the season of greatest aridity, (dryness) and the hottest midday sunshine and that the balance of the year has a fair proportion of rainfall for the successful growth of those plants, adapted to their locations and seasons. It also must not be forgotten that climate will not yield theories however plausible, but theories to be of any value, must conform to climate and practice must be goverened accordingly. The guiding star climate must always be in sight and always kept in view if the agricul-turist would march in the way of success.

How to grow and care for an orange grove or orchard in California, Spain or Italy, where irrigation is an absolute necessity, can be of little value to men in Florida where climatic conditions are varient (different,) the same remark may also be applicable to the cultivation, gathering and handling of fruits and vegetables for the markets. If the climate of some other region requires lemons to be gather-ed when they can be passed through an iron ring of a given size that is not a reason why the lemons of Florida, that will grow to nearly twice the size without deteriorating, should be passed through the same ring, so too, a descrip-tion of how to grow an orange orchard or handle the fruit in Porti Rica or Jamacia, would, to the common reader be equally uninstructive unless the climatic differences between those places and Florida were also kept in view. Climate is the keynote with which the whole must accord, or there will be discords innumerable.

Florida has its own climate which must remain as per-manent as earth itself. It cannot be taken away, and people must conform to it, or failure will certainly ensue.''

Much, if not all of the above letter is true in a general sense, but much more may, and can be said about the seasons and climate of Florida.

The thermometer seldom ranges below 30 de-grees above zero. In January 1886, it however got below twenty. This is said to have been the hardest freeze that ever occurred since 1835, when it was about as cold. The last freeze destroyed

all the fruits of Florida, except the oranges and it
hurt them. All the citrus trees were frozen to the
ground. (roots not killed) except the orange trees,
many of which were not hurt at all, while many
others lost their foliage and some in exposed places
were frozen to the ground This, however, seems
to be an exception as this kind of weather very
seldom occurs. As a general thing in the winter
season the thermometer ranges from about thirty
to seventy above zero, and in summer from about
sixty-five to ninety-five above zero. Sometimes,
however, the mercury clinbs up to one hundred
and even above that. About this time the weather
is pretty hot, but while the days are hot, nights
comparatively cool, there being usually a breeze
that makes it pleasant, but sometimes this breeze
fails to come, or you may be so placed that you
cannot get the advantage of it. At such times if
you were here you would think the nights pretty
warm also. There is not much cloudy weather.
Rains come in showers and are of short duration,
then sunshine. A day in Florida that the sun does
not shine brightly some part of the day, would be an
anomaly. Fogs are almost unknown; the air
seems to be pure and very dry—indeed very dry,
when we consider the amount of water with which
we are surrounded.

The climate in the winter about compares with
the climate of New York and Pennsylvania in
November and April, leaving out the cold rains.

The winter seasons here, are as a usual thing, rather dry; that is there is not much rainfall. Occasionally a wet spell about the latter part of March or in early April, then usually very dry until late in June, when the rainy season sets in, which usually lasts about three months, during which time scarcely a day passes without one or more showers of rain, and some of these are very heavy, and usually accompanied with thunder and lightning, and oh! such vivid and bright lightning. When these showers occur at night, as they frequently do, it seems sometimes as if the whole heavens was lighted up with continuous streams of liquid fire, and the thunder so loud and sharp the ground seems to tremble and shake, and it actually does. It is grand and sublime to see the lightning and hear the thunder, but it is rather unpleasant to have it so near you. What are called settled rains never occur here, though sometimes it will rain right along for as much as a half a day at a time and when it rains there is no drizzle to it, but a genuine pour down and done with it. Should one of these big rains occur, then look out for high waters.

Low lands are converted into lakes and ponds in the shortest possible space of time, and if you chance to be in some of the flat portions of the State, (and the greater part is flat) you will begin to think that Florida is nearly all lakes, ponds and swamps, sure enough, but on the contrary should you visit Florida in a dry time, you certainly would think they have a good deal of dry land there, and so we have a good part of the year, however some, and a large sum too, that is dry in some parts of the year, in other parts of the same year are several feet under water. This kind of land is not of much account for anything but pasture for stock and not worth much for that, simply because not much of anything but bramble grows on it.

Florida is a very pleasant State to live in during the winter season provided you have plenty of money to enable you to secure good and comfortable quarters or to build you a place to suit yourself. With all the necessaries, luxuries and delicacies of life can be procured here at all times. (What are not grown and raised here are shipped here from the North and other places,) but sometimes, and nearly always, the prices are enormously high and the very many tropical fruits and berries that you expect to see growing here in abundance, you will be rather surprised to find that many of them are brought here from foreign parts and a great many things that are grown here that you had expected to find common and low in price, when you discover the facts you will find that many of these things had to have great care and nursing to bring them to even partial perfection, and the price asked will be more than the same fruits, vegetables and berries could be bought

for in Northern markets, even at the same time of
the year. Almost all the substantial food we eat
in Florida, is shipped here from the North—flour,
butter, bacon, Irish potatoes, apples, corn meal,
&c. To feed our horses we use hay from the
North, even from New England. Oats and corn
are all shipped here, and we have even to ship our
chicken feed.

True we raise oranges, lemons, limes, grape
fruit, grapes, sweet potatoes, water melons, cante-
lopes, tomatoes, beans, cucumbers, mulberries and
strawberries. Oh yes! we fairly bask in strawberries and cream. The cheapest strawberries I
saw in Florida, were twenty-five cents a box,
(about a pint,) and small at that, from the holidays to about the first of April, they usually sell
at about one dollar a box. Cheap, *is not it so?*
You see that persons with plenty of money can indulge in strawberries and cream, when they can
get the cream. It costs forty cents a quart; blue
milk from fifteen to twenty cents a quart, depends
a little on how badly you want it. For people
that do not have a great deal of filthy lucre, strawberries and cream is no good in Florida.

Now take snap beans. These grow well here
and are plenty in the month of April, and sell right
along at about one dollar a peck, About this time
the Irish potatoes that grow in Florida come into
market at about the same price as beans. Onions
by the bunch, (about half a dozen little ones in a

bunch) sell at from fifteen to twenty cents a bunch. Red beets are very hard to grow here, and sell very high. Lettuce, cabbage and all other garden trucks sell at about the proportion of the above figures. About the first of June green corn, watermelons and tomatoes come into market and sell about as follows: very small corn per dozen, twenty to fifty cents; until watermelons come become plenty, they bring a dollar a piece—they get cheaper about July first. Tomatoes sell for a dollar a peck, and not very good even at that price. The only things that are really cheap are turnips and sweet potatoes, and these sell all the time from forty to ninety cents a bushel. So it is pretty plain to be seen that unless you raise these things yourself or have plenty of money, you might as well be anywhere else as in Florida, so far as enjoying the eating of them is concerned. Notwithstanding all this, the climate of Florida in winter as compared with the Northern States, is delightful. In the summer I prefer being in a climate that the heat is not quite so great, and I have a very strong impression that should the readers ever spend a summer in Florida, they will agree with me long before the summer is ended.

SOMETHING ABOUT ORANGES, ETC.

There are several varieties of oranges. They ripen from October to February, according as they are early or late varieties. They are not easily shaken from the tree and after being matured and

fully ripe, they stick so tightly to their fastenings
that the branches to which they grow are frequently broken off in attempting to pull them.   When, or
in gathering the oranges, the gatherer fastens a
sack or basket, made for the purpose, in front of
him with straps or strings passing around his
shoulders, and with a pair of snips (scissors) or a
knife with a hooked blade, thus equipped he
mounts a step ladder after placing it in proper position about the tree and gathers the golden fruit,
depositing each orange in the receptacle separately.   This gathering of oranges is a kind of a trade
and an expert will thus gather many thousands in
a single day, when many another who does not
understand the business will not be able to gather
as many hundred in the same length of time.   Pro-
fessional orange gatherers work or gather by the
hundred and some of them do nothing else.   They
make (earn) enough money during the gathering
seasons to keep them the balance of the year.   Occasionally you will see two crops on the same tree,
(ripe and green) and very frequently you will see
the tree bloom out for a new crop and have plenty
of ripe fruit on at the same time, yet they produce
but one full crop a year and not as many suppose
that the tree is an everbearer, that is that they are
producing fruit all the time.   I never saw an
orange tree that was an everbearer and the reason
you occasionally hear as above written, is because
of the tenacity with which the fruit sticks to or ad-

heres to the tree and not having been gathered. If, however, the tree or fruit is unsound, the fruit loses this tenacity and falls to the ground, hence you never see an orange grower eat an orange that has not been cut or taken directly from the tree; notwithstanding some unscrupulous persons will ship wind falls, that is oranges that have dropped from the trees, from being diseased in some way. These oranges can always be told in this way and in no other. The absence of a small part of the stem on which the orange grew, is very suspicious. All first-class oranges have this small part of the stem firmly attached and it is almost impossible to get it off without injuring the rind or skin of it.

The orange trees as well as all the citrus family, is an evergreen, that is it is always full of green leaves. Should the foliage become destroyed, as is the case sometimes by frost, worms, or insects, it will soon put out a new foliage. The tree is all the time (very slowly) casting off the old and making new wood and foliage, yet you scarcely ever see an orange leaf under the trees.

AN ORANGE ORCHARD.

An orange grove is planted something after the style of an apple orchard (in the North) and by planting three year old budded trees that have had proper care and by planting properly and giving them all the attendance necessary and fertilizing them all they will take; if on the right kind of soil, you may expect, and will get a few oranges the third or fourth year after planting. Your orange grove must be cared for just like a garden, and the more you work, manure or fertilize it, the better it will do, and if you fail to give it proper attention, it will show it very quickly. About the seventh or eighth year after planting, if it has had the proper kind of attention, it will begin to pay you, that is you will begin to get fruit and when it once begins to make returns, (the older the grove gets the more it will return) provided you always keep fertilizing and giving it proper attention. You might just as well fatten an animal and after he is fat, expect him to remain so without feed or attention as to plant an orange grove and bring it into bearing and then expect it to continue bearing without giving it the same attention that you did to bring it into that condition. In this respect orange trees are very sensative and are more like corn or vegetables; they show neglect or good care almost immediately. The man or person who expects to get an orange grove by simply planting the trees and then let them take care of themselves will only reap vexation and disappointment. You might just as well plant corn in a clover field without ploughing, and then expect a crop of corn without any further attention, the one would be just about as likely to succeed as the other. Work, attention and fertilizing are the three main points in making an orange grove.

From what I have seen, know and learned

about this orange business. in my judgement there
are very few orange groves in the State that have
ever paid the cost of bringing into bearing and
keeping up. Do not understand that all who have
planted groves have lost money—very far from it.
On the contrary, nearly every person that has
planted groves and given them any kind of care
or attention at all, have made money by the oper-
ation of planting and starting groves, and also
made money by bringing them into bearing. not
in the fruit however. It is done about in this way :
Purchase five acres of land within a mile or two of
a smart town for fifty dollars per acre. have it
cleared and fenced, (or do it yourself) and planted
for say one hundred dollars per acre more ; be
careful to have nice thriving trees ; have them set
out in June, about the beginning of the rainy season ; have the ground in prime condition ; all the
trees, stumps and roots taken out. and make it look
like a garden ; trees start to grow at once, being
aided by the wet weather and some powerful fertilizer ; watch and attend to them carefully, keeping
off all sprouts and suckers : watch the orange dog,
a kind of worm something like the worm that gets
on seed parsnips in the North—they destroy the
foliage ; also keep off the ants and all other insects
that infest orange trees ; wash the trees occasionally with whale-oil soap, and don't forget your fertilizer, and by the first of November you will have
a new growth of wood from three to five feet, and

the trees will look beautiful. Now this whole business up to this time will not have cost over two
hundred dollars per acre, including your own work
and all expenses. Some man from the North or
elsewhere, comes along with more dollars than
knowledge and he wants an orange grove, you
ask him a thousand dollars per acre or five thous-
and dollars for the whole tract; you show him the
big growth. He wants to know how old these
trees are, when they were planted, how much attention and how much fertilizer you have used.
Of course you tell him all about it, making as
much out of the growth as you can and enlarging
on the very short time in which they put on the
this very heavy growth; keep the fertilizer and the
attention paid to the trees as much in the background as possible; you will show up all the good
qualities of your country, or your place in particular; do not however seem to want to sell, but
show by figures and calculations what your grove
will produce, (no probabilities about this) as soon
as it comes into bearing; you can easily figure up
that in six or eight years your grove will produce
the interest on from eight to ten thousand dollars
per acre and maybe you can get him to believe it.
Whether you do or not, he does not know how
much truth you have told him, and he will not be
likely to find out very soon unless he should happen to buy and come to Florida to live. However,
if you have played your part well, you have him

fascinated by this time, for this orange business is fascinating to a stranger; he will very probably make you an offer for your grove of perhaps one half of what you asked him; you of course could not think for a moment of taking any such offer, but before the matter is settled you have sold your grove for seven hundred and fifty dollars per acre acre and have thus made over two thousand dollars clear money, and he has the grove. This is not a bad speculation for you, but unless he stays right there and attends to his grove just as well as you did, he cannot help but lose money. I know of a case just exactly like this and know the parties, but suppose you do not sell the first fall or winter, there is such a thing as dwarfing and pushing an orange tree, that it will bear a few oranges the second year from the bud. You are likely to have a few of these kind of trees, and if so, you will be sure to call particular attention to them and they do look nice, and almost certain to attract and fascinate, and many times you make money by not selling the first year, but then it is generally all the worse for the END MAN. You certainly have made money by planting an orange grove. The man that now owns it, has his to make yet. My judgement is that there is more money made out of orange groves before they come into bearing than there is afterward. I mean clear money. There are many, very many things about this orange business that the uninitiated know but little about.

However, with all the tricks thrown in, some of the finest oranges raised in the world are grown in Florida, and it is a nice business and many honorable men and women are engaged in the business of growing oranges and orange trees in Florida, and many of them are doing well, while others, and many of them are ready and willing to sell out as soon as the right man puts in his appearance. You can always buy orange groves.

LEMONS AND LIMES

Are not, as a general thing planted in groves, but in odd corners and sometimes between the rows of orange trees. They are more of a bush than a tree and come into bearing in two or three years from budding. Florida produces lemons and limes of a good quality, but not of the best. These trees or bushes are very tender and a frost of any severity at all, ruins the fruit for that year, hence the fruit growers do not cultivate them to any great extent. There is, however a large, rough, thick skinned lemon that stands about as much freezing as an orange tree. They are not of a very good quality and not much accounted of.

CITRON TREES OR BUSHES.

This fruit is more of a novelty than anything else. It is a large fruit and somewhat bell shaped, some of them weighing as much as ten pounds. Whether it is the citron of commerce or not, I have not been able to learn, nor have I been able to earn of any person making any use of them whatever. The trees or bushes are rather small, something like a lemon tree. The branches are very tough and elastic, and the weight of the fruit bends the boughs until the fruit touches the ground.

GRAPE FRUIT. *(Shaddocks)*

This seems to be a kind of an orange. It grows on a tree that looks like an orange tree, and unless you saw the fruit, you would say the tree was an orange tree. The fruit is very full of juice and is used in various ways, as lemons for drink and making PIES. Jelly is also made of grape fruit, and by many persons it is eaten the same as an orange. It is not so sour as a lemon, but much more so than a good orange. In size it is very much larger than the largest orange; one or two grape fruit trees is all any person wants on his place. They ripen and stick on the trees about like an orange. They are not often shipped North for the reason that there is not much money made by handling them. The tree grows as large, if not larger than an orange tree and bears heavily every year, if kept in good condition.

GUAVA.

The tree is of a bush character and grows something like a quince does when left alone (in the North.) It does not grow tall, but branches out from the ground. I have seen them from twelve to fifteen feet in diameter through the branches, six or eight feet from the ground, and not more than ten or twelve feet high. These bushes are not hard to propagate and when once started, need but very little care and they bear an abundant crop every year (when not frozen.) The fruit is about the size of a small lemon, and shaped a little like a mandrake or May apple and is very full of seeds, something like tomato seeds, only larger.   The fruit is used for a great many purposes, and a great many persons like them to eat right off the bush and nearly every person becomes very fond of them after they once get the taste properly.   They are used for jellies and jams, for which they are excellent, as the jellies and jams can be flavored to taste.   They make excellent pies and not a bad desert in the absence of something better.   The bushes bear the second or third year from planting.

PINE APPLES.

These are rather hard to raise, being a tropical fruit they cannot stand frost, hence must be protected in winter.   A good many are raised, however, in the southern part of Florida.   Under protection they mature from the planting in about twenty-one months.   The ground is prepared as for cabbage ; the plants are set in rows about two feet apart, and the rows are about the same distance apart ; they must be carefully cultivated and fertilized, and no grass or weeds allowed to grow among them ; cultivated like cabbage.   After a proper time a kind of spike shoots up from the centre of the plant, something like a poppy head or tulip flower, with a bulb on top; this bulb is the pine apple. which grows and enlarges and finally ripens. Each plant produces but one apple then dies, but while it is bearing this apple it is at the same time rattooning or throwing out several other plants from the old root, which in turn, each bears an apple. So you see a pine apple bed is self-propagating, and once planted is there indefinitely If proper care is taken of them, all you have to do is to see that it does not become too thickly set with stalks, in which case the fruit would be small. After the bed or orchard is properly started and cared for and well protected in winter, you can, and will have ripe fruit the whole year around, as there seems to be no special season of the year in which they ripen. so that after a very few years, you will have pine apples all the time in all stages of growth and of all sizes. The pine apple stock is very rough, and in working among them the hands, arms and legs must be protected with leather, in order to keep your skin and flesh from being torn and lacerated. Plants are obtained from the roots and also from small suckers that shoot out from the base of the apple. If the top of the apple be cut off and planted, it will also grow and in due course of time produce another apple.

BANANAS.

This is also a tropical fruit and plant but partially acclimated to Florida, and when planted in places not too much exposed, fruits tolerably well.

The least bit of a freeze stops the fruiting.   It
is grown for ornament in nearly all gardens and
lots in the State, particularly in the southern part.
It grows to the height of twenty or more feet in
good soil.   Its foliage or leaves are from two to
six feet long and when flattened out will measrue as
much as two feet in width ; the leaves have a rib
or stem running through the middle the long way
of the leaf, thus it appears to be double, drooping
from the stem.   When the stock is ready to fruit,
it sends up a strong stem from the centre of the
stock, after the nature of the pine apple.   This
stem is from one to three inches in diameter ; on
the outer or extreme end of this stem or spike is
what is called the blow ; this is in shape a good
deal like an ear of corn and about the size, the
layers answering to the husk on corn ; it is red and
when this blow opens, as it always does, is very
beautiful ; when the blow begins to open then the
butt or lower end of this spike begins to, and does
throw out segments partially around it, which
seems to divide, each pushing out a small yellow
flower ; this is the blossom   Each blossom is the
end of the fruit, which grows very much like a
cucumber, in that the blossom is on the end of the
fruit.   In a short time another of these sequents
forms and the process is repeated again and again
until from a dozen to three hundred bananas are
formed on this stem or spike.   When the blow first
makes its appearance, its weight curves the stem

and by the time the fruit is well formed the top of the bunch is toward the ground. A stock only bears one bunch and then dies, but like the pine apple, is self-propagating. sending out rattoons or suckers from the roots, which in turn produce fruit. The stock has the nature of corn, being very porous, but not jointed, and are sometimes as much as eight inches in diameter within a foot of the ground. They will grow in almost any kind of soil. but do much the best in low lands. They will grow without fertilizer, but will do better with it. They propagate in Florida entirely from the roots; they will not mature seed outside of a purely tropical climate; there are several varieties of them some of which are much better than others; very few, if any bananas are shipped from Florida; about all that grow here are consumed in the State.

GRAPES.

The are several varieties of natural grapes, none of which amount to much except the "Scuppernong," which is a very fair grape, especially when no better is to be had. There are several varieties of grapes growing wild in the Hammocks that are something like the fox grapes of the North. only smaller. Grapes other than the scuppernong do not seem to do much good in this climate.

PEACHES.

There are two kinds of peaches that can be

raised in Florida.   The Peen-to or Pinto is a small
flat, fair peach; it does fairly here and ripens in
early June.   The honey peach is small and yellowish; it is very sweet and ripens a little later.   The
kind and varieties of peaches that grow in the
North, do not seem to grow here-   There is, however, a new peach called the Bidwell, about which,
just now a big blow is being made.   I have not
seen any of these peaches, but if one-half that is
said about them be true, they will revolutionize the
fruit growing business in this State.   They are
said to even ripen earlier than the Peen-to, and it
is further said that they are worth in the New York
market about twenty-seven dollars a bushel.   The
reader must bear in mind that we do not vouch for
this Bidwell peach, but simply write what is said
about them by those who are interested in the sale
if the Bidwell peach trees and what is published
on the papers by those otherwise interested in this
variety of peach.   One thing is pretty certain, and
that is that time will test this peach as well as many
other things in Florida.

PEARS.

The Leconte is the only pear that can be raised
in Florida.   This grows something like the SECKEL
pear of the North and somewhat larger; it has a
fine flavor, (rather too sweet.)   The trees are
propagated from cuttings.

PLUMS.

It is said that plums grow wild in some parts of

the State. I have seen the so-called Persian plum which grow on a tree something like the horse chestnut tree. The fruit is about the size of a green gage and is much relished by some people. There is to me very little, if any plum taste about them.

PERSIMMONS.

There are two varieties here. The common persimmon of the North flourishes here and produces abundant crops, but are of very little use. The other variety has been brought here from Japan; when ripe, is rather a fancy fruit, and is relished by everbody. The fruit is yellow when ripe, and is usually about three inches long and about one inch in diameter, having but few seeds, and they are very small. The fruit is very slightly astringent, even when very ripe, not enough so, however to make it objectional. The trees are propagated by budding into wild persimmon stocks and from seed; the trees raised from seed must be grafted or budded to insure good fruit. Shaddocks have been described under the name of grape fruit, as both names mean about the same fruit. A further description would be superfluous.

POMEGRANATES

Are grown in some places; they are like the citron, more ornamental than useful: the tree or rather bush is very beautiful, and the fruit in shape resembles a half grown quince in appearance and size, the colors however are reddish.

BERRIES.

Strawberries are the principal, and in fact about the only cultivated berry in Florida. They need no particular description as every person knows all about strawberries. I may say that by proper cultivation and planting at the right season, these berries may be had or the crop continued from the holidays until about the first of July. The principal crop, however, is made during March and April. In order to obtain berries as early *or late* as the holidays, the plants must be set out in June or early in July. Planting them at this time of the year, they require the greatest kind of care, mulcing and protection from the hot sun, and by keeping away from them all grass and weeds and using the proper fertilizer, you may succeed in getting some berries, provided the frost don't kill them. You will not get much of a crop, but what you do get will be worth from two to five dollars a box in New York—no not worth that amount, but will bring that price. If only a few quarts are thus raised, and they are, it answers first-rate for an advertisement of what can be done in the State, and will find big accounts of strawberries raised in the open air in Florida. These accounts never give the " modus operandi " of raising the berries To make a success of raising strawberries in Florida, they must be planted in September or October, the ground being first well prepared and fertilized, then if properly attended, you can expect, and will get a fair crop of berries the following March and April. Sometimes you can begin to pick ripe strawberries in February and from the same plants get a few berries as late as July. The berries do not ripen all at once as they do in the North, but continue ripening all along throughout the season, of say three or four months, or even longer from the time the first berries come until the last are done. These old plants produce but very few berries the second year, so of necessity you must plant new beds each year or reset the old ones. The price of strawberries here is about the same as it is in the New York market all the time, so you must either raise your berries, have plenty of money, or do without, just as it happens.

HUCKLE AND BLACKBERRIES

Of an inferior quality grow wild in Hammocks and low lands, and in season are peddled around as they are in the North. They bring from ten to twenty-five cents a quart, depends a little on how badly you want them.

CURRANTS, RASPBERRIES, GOOSE-BERRIES, ELDERBERRIES AND CHERRIES.

I have seen none of these, nor have I seen any person that did see them, notwithstanding, it is said some of each grow in the State, and I know no reason why they should not grow here at least as well as strawberries.

MULBERRIES

Grow wild in the Hammocks, and they seem to be of the same variety as the Northern. There is also a tame or cultivated mulberry that is very large and ripens in April. They, however, are not very valuable as they are rather soft and taste-less.

VEGETABLE AND TUBERS.

Cucumbers and sweet potatoes are perfectly at home in Florida; about all that is to be done to get a crop of either, is to prepare the ground and plant the seed. You can either plant the whole sweet potato or the draws (plants) or pieces of the sweet potato vine, and with very little cultivation you will get a fair crop—better cultivation will produce a better crop. Cucumbers do the best when planted in February or March. If planted much later the hot sun interferes with their maturing. Sweet potatoes should be planted the latter part of May or early in June to make the best crop, however, the can be planted at almost any other time of the year, and generally do well; the crop may remain in the ground for a long time without injury. This, however, is a lazy way of keeping them. The right way is to dig them, take them out of the ground and bank them, (put them in pits) as they do Irish potatoes in the North. Many people dig them and put them on piles, cover lightly with sand, then cover all with palmetto bushes or moss. As a general thing enough of seed is left in the ground to produce a crop the next season, and frequently the second crop is almost as good the first, without much, if any additional labor.

WATER AND MUSH MELONS.

These can be, and are raised here by the million. They, however. must have a good deal of attention and the ground must be well fertilized and the seed planted at the proper time, which is in February and never later than March for general crop. Start the plants with plenty of good fertilizer, watch the cut worms, (they do have cut worms in Florida) and insects, keep your plants and vines growing vigorously, one hill to each—ten feet square is plenty thick enough, and if you have more than three stocks in a hill, it is too thick. Mush melons may be planted a little closer. All things being favorable, the melons produced in Florida cannot be surpassed in the known world.

IRISH POTATOES.

The Irish potatoes that are raised in Florida, cannot be classed as first quality by any means, although there are some fair potatoes raised here. When planted at the proper time, and January, by my observation, is the right time. As a general thing Irish potatoes that are raised here have a watery nature and many of them are black inside. The whole of it is, raising Irish potatoes in Florida is not a success, and I do not think ever will be.

CABBAGE.

Cabbage on certain kinds of soil, grows very well, as for instance on reclaimed marsh land or low hammock, provided you can keep the cutworms insects, and cabbage worms off. I have seen no very large heads of cabbage grown in Florida, but have heard ot them. I have however seen hundreds that were called fine cabbage; if the heads being small and solid made it fine, then the saying is true. As a general thing the heads weigh from one to four pounds, although I have seen others that weighed five and six pounds.

ONIONS.

Onions are not a success, still on good land, with care and plenty of fertilizer and planting wide apart fair onions can be raised here.

TURNIPS.

Turnips of all kinds grow pretty well. Fertilizer helps them wonderfully.

RED BEETS.

Red beets for some cause not known to the writer, does not grow here except in special localities, and in no locality do they amount to much.

SQUASHES AND PUMPKINS.

As a general crop are a partial success. Egg plants in certain localities, with care and plenty of fertilizer, make a fair crop.

TOMATOES.

As a general crop with ordinary care and a little fertilizer, make a good crop. especially the small round cluster tomato. To be a success, they should be planted very early in the season, say the last of December or first of January. Be sure to protect when there is danger of frost.

CORN.

This can be raised on cow penned land or with plenty of fertilizer. February is the time to plant, and you will then have mutton corn (roasting ears) in early June. A crop of corn yielding, say twenty bushels to the acre, is considered a pretty good crop for Florida. Not much is raised except for table use.

COTTON.

In the Northern part of the State considerable cotton is raised, both Sea Island and Short Staple, and does very well.

WHEAT AND RYE.

Rye and wheat will not mature here. There is some of both sowed, epecially rye for pasture.

OATS.

A very good crop can be made with plenty of fertilizer in the Northern part of the State.

BEANS.

Beans when properly planted, cultivated and fertilized, make an excellent crop, especially wax and snap varieties. Many thousands of bushels of beans are raised in Florida every year and shipped to the Northern markets. Beans are one of the staple crops of the State.

COW PEAS.

These are a kind of a small bean generally sown broadcast on new land.   As a first crop, it is said they sweeten the land, that is takes out the wildness, and makes land productive.   These cow peas are frequently plowed down, thus acting as a fertilizer, other times they are left stand until about half ripe, then cut and cured like hay. In this shape they are excellent food for stock, they do not seem to impoverish the land, but rather to enrich it.   These cow peas are very rough food for man.

HOSS (HORSE) BEANS.

These are grown for ornament and shade. They are climbers.   I have seen them climb a pine tree for forty feet; their foliage is very dense, and the bean pods are as much as a foot long, having usually twelve large beans in each pod.   I know of no use for the beans.

HOPS.

These are not grown in Florida to my knowledge.

ASPARAGUS.

Have neither saw any or heard of any in the State.

HORSE RADDISH.

The same as Asparagus.

RADDISHES.

These grow quickly when fertilizer is used, but get spongy very soon.

TOBACCO.

It is said tobacco will grow well in places, but I have neither seen the places or the tobacco growing.

CASAVA.

Casava is said to be a sure and profitable crop. This is the root out of which tapioca is made. I have heard of it, but know of none growing in the State.

PEA NUTS, PINDARS OR GOUBERS.

These grow well and yield abundantly if properly planted, cultivated, cared for and fertilized.

CASTOR BEANS.

These grow to be quite large, (that is the stocks) I have seen them as much as six inches in diameter near the ground. These stocks were all frozen dead in the heavy freeze of January 1886, and it will be several years before such large stocks will be seen again. A castor bean stock will naturally live and bear beans for several years in succession, not killed by frost or otherwise. Many orange growers plant or sow castor beans in their groves for the purpose of keeping down other weeds and grass and to shade the ground, thereby acting as a kind of mulch and yet letting the air circulate freely on the surface of the ground. The bean stocks are said to act as a fertilizer for the orange trees in that way. How this is I do not know, but I do know that where you see an orange grove thickly set with castor beans, the trees look nice and thrifty and seem to be doing well.

BUCKWHEAT.

I never saw or heard of any buckwheat growing in the State.

RICE.

A very little rice is grown. It is sown in rows about eighteen inches apart and thickly in the row. When it first comes up it looks like oats and unless you knew what it was, you would say it was oats, until it shoots out the heads, which are a little different from oats. being much stiffer and more upright, Rice like most other grain, grows taller or shorter in the straw, according to the quality of the land on which it is raised.

FIGS.

Nearly every fruit grower in Florida has a few fig trees or bushes. These, as far as I can see, are like some other fruits grown here, more ornamental than useful. While some people eat the figs right from the tree and pretend to say they are good and palatable, I would about as soon eat oak apples. I do not know but that these figs could be prepared in some way and made palatable and salable, but as they are now, they might as well be marked N. G. However they do very well to talk about by persons who are much interested in this Eldorado. They can say figs grow there also.

NATIVE GRASSES.

The native grasses of Florida are nearly all of a

course, rough character and do not seem to possess much nutriment, with very few exceptions. Among them all, the crab grass seems to be the best. This is a joint grass and grows very thickly on the ground, and when trampled upon, wherever a joint touches the ground, it grows fast and forms a new stock ; it also produces seed in abundance, so you see it reproduces both from the tops and by rooting from the joints. It somewhat resembles blue grass when it is standing straight up, but very much coarser and rougher. Cattle and horses eat it readily and greedily and stock fatten on it alone. When not grazed off, it will grow to the height of two or three feet and in many places covers the ground as thick as it can stand. If mown or cut just before the seed ripens and well cured , it will make very good hay. Cattle and horses will eat it when well cured and seem to relish it about as well as when green. Unfortunately this grass grows only in certain localities and is only available for pasture, and hay for a comparatively short time. It does not remain green all the year around, but it cures on the stock and becomes hard and dry, as do most of the native grasses here, and then stock either will nor or cannot eat it. Wire grass is a native. When young and tender stock eat it, but it soon begins to have the appearance of running briars, becomes hard and woody, when nothing but goats can eat it. It is good for nothing then that I know of but to harbor

and breed red bugs or jiggers. There is also a
native grass that is more general than any other
in the State. It has the appearance of what people
in the North call "white top," a grass that grows
in old natural meadows in the North, and is as
thick as the hair on a wooly dog, near and on the
ground and hardly ever grows over a foot high.
This grass is fine in the stem, and remains green
the greater part of the year, hence it is the main
dependence of the stock raiser. Then there is a
very fine grass (that is fine or small in the stock)
and short that grows in old roads and old fields.
Cattle only eat this when they can get nothing
else ; then there is what is called bunch grass, something after the nature of what is called sour grass
in the North, only it grows in bunches. The
western man will understand when I say it compares in appearance with the roughest kind of June
grass ; then there is what is called saw grass.
This, when young and tender, is much relished
by cattle, but soon becomes hard and the teeth on
the blades so sharp and hard that cattle will not
even go near it ; then there is the marsh swamp and
bull grass and a kind of grass that grows in the
bottom of shallow lakes and ponds. These latter
remain green the whole year around and are the
only source of feed for stock in the winter season,
except the scrub and saw palmetto, which is the
roughest kind of forage, unless hay or dry feed is
provided, hence the cattle get very poor in the

winter and toward spring and many of them die
from sheer starvation. There are some other
native grasses and plenty of weeds, mosses, pig-
weed, &c., that would be useles and of no advantage to any person to describe.

BERMUDA GRASS.

This grass is a foreigner, imported from Bermuda, but took to the soil of Florida at once. It
seems to be very closely related to the crab grass,
but of a finer quality. It is also a joint grass and
propagates the same way from the roots and joints,
but produces no seed, hence to start it you must
plant the roots or joints, either of which will grow
in any kind of soil or even in pure sand, and when
once started, it is there just as long as you want it,
and sometimes longer, for should you want to get
rid of it, you will find a larger job than it was to
start it in the first place. This Bermuda grass is
better in quality and equally as good in quantity,
and answers every purpose that the crab grass
does, with the advantage that it will grow anywhere or place where there is soil or sand of any
kind, which the crab grass will not do.

TIMOTHY AND CLOVER.

There is none growing anywhere in the State
that I know of, nor do I think there ever will be.
The soil is not the kind to produce either the one
or the other.

ALFALFA OR GERMAN CLOVER.

I have heard it said that some man got a few

seeds of it, planted it in his garden and it sprouted, came up and after it got to be a few inches high, had an advertisement put in the papers to the effect that Alfalfa was the coming grass for Florida. He knew there was no mistake about it that he had the thing itself growing luxuriously on his place, when the facts were exactly as stated above. This stem alone will give you some idea of how Florida is "boomed" up by those interested. Persons reading the above mentioned notice a thousand miles Northward, where clover, timothy and Alfalfa are grown in large fields, you would at once take it for granted that this man away down in Florida had acres of Alfalfa growing on his farm, and it is a well known fact that this grass is a great producer and you would at once conclude, "well if Alfalfa grows that way down there, there surely need be no scarcity of either pasture, fodder or hay,' when the facts were simply a few stocks had been coaxed to grow a few inches Now it has been said that "truth is mighty and will prevail. " I reckon the saying is true, when the truth, the whole truth and nothing but the truth is said or written. Now in this Alfalfa case the truth and nothing but the truth was written or advertised. the Alfalfa seeds were planted, germinated and grew, but it was told in such a way that it would mislead almost any person that was not, at least partially acquainted with the circumstances, climate or country. The fact is a crop of Alfalfa cannot be grown in Florida, no more than timothy, clover or any of the Northern tame or field grasses, for the reason that the season, soil, climate and all other natural condi ions are against it, just as they are against growing wheat and other cereals that require the seed to be frozen in the ground, or the ground frozen and prepared before the seed is put into it. It will be well enough to theorize, say and write that there is no reason known why thus and so can't be done, but there are reasons and good ones, too, why certain things cannot be done. Notwithstanding all our theories, speculations or imaginations about them, if the natural conditions are not favorable in the end, you will have your labor for your pains and reap only disappointment and vexation. Theories and imaginations to amount to anything at all, must conform to the nature of the thing or subject theorized upon, otherwise they are valueless.

WILD FLOWERS—TREES.

Among the wild flowers, the Magnolia for size and sweetness, may be called the queen. These flowers when in full bloom, resemble an enormous cabbage rose, only they are perfectly white. A large magnolia in full bloom is a sight when once seen, will never be forgotten ; the most delightful perfume fills the air for many rods around the tree. Many of the flowers are more than a foot in diameter when in full bloom. There is this peculiarity about them, while they are perfectly white, and remain so while on the tree and after they are taken

off, unless your finger or any part of your flesh
touches them, when the spot touched immediately
turns red and remains so. The tree remains in
bloom for several weeks, but produces no kind of
either nuts or fruit, nothing but kind of cone. It
is an evergreen, but only blooms once a year, and
that in April or early May. There are some other
trees that produce flowers, but when you have
once seen the Magnolia, all the other flowering
trees dwindle into such insignificance that a description here seems to be superfluous.

WILD VINES.

The trumpet flower and the honey suckle grow
wild here in the Hammocks and produce large and
beautiful flowers. Some of the trumpet flowers are
as much as fifteen to eighteen inches in length,
while the honey suckles bloom abundantly· Very
many of the flowering vines and shrubbery of the
North grow wild in this State.

FLOWERING SHRUBBERY.

The wild Jassamine is perhaps the grandest.
You will see great masses of this in the Hammocks
literally covered with flowers in early summer.
The flowers of many are variegated, while others
are white, and indeed you can find Jassamine of
almost any color. It is said the flowers are poisonous, but of this I could get no certain knowledge
There are many other shrubs and small bushes
that produce flowers, some nice and large, others
very small and tiny. There is a bush that grows

to the height of several feet and produces a purple
and white flower. The flower both before and
after it opens is covered with a kind of stick sub-
sance something like syrup or honey. The flies
seem to like this substance, but woe to the fly that
a lights on flower bud or blossom ; his feet immediately become fastened and in his efforts to get
away, his wings become fastened also and in a
very short space of time the fly is dead. This
bush is plenty in some localities and where they
grow you do not find the flies so plentiful. If you
break off the bush that have flower buds and blossoms on them and place them, or hang them in
your horse, in a very short time they will be full
of dead flies. I know of no name for this bush or
flour but FLY CATCHER.

MARYGOLDS.

Marygolds of the reddish variety, grow wild
here. There are hundreds of flowers of about all
sorts and sizes growing in the timber and low
lands of Florida, some of which are very beautiful,
and very many of them are tiny, and but very few
of the wild flowers have any perceptable perfume
in them,

CULTIVATED FLOWERS.

Ore pinks, petumas, nearly all varieties of
roses, four o'clock, tulips, peonies, asters, chrysan-
themums and any, and nearly all other kinds and
varieties of flowers that you may fancy can be
grown in Florida, provided you have the patience,

time and money to buy and attend to them. Many
of the flowers here are like tropical and semi-trop-
cal fruits and shrubbery in the North. They can
be had with proper care, attention and protection.
With a very few exceptions the natural and wild
flowers of Florida are neither plentier or prettier
than they are in the North, and yet it is called the
"Land of Sunshine and Flowers." It could be
called the Land of Sand and Shower with rather
more propriety than the other, but there is not so
very much in a name after all, particularly when
the truth is known.

LILLIES AND CALLA LILLIES

Of nearly every kind and color grow wild; so
do flags. These latter grow in some lands, some
of which are very pretty.

FLOWERING MOSSES.

Such as are cultivated in the North, are here,
treated as weeds, and are considerable of a nuis-
ance in the gardens.

EVERGREEN TREES

Are all of the citrus family, such as orange,
lemon, shaddock, lime, &c. The magnolia bay,
live oak, turkey oak, water oak, palmetto, mangrove, pine and some others.

DECIDUOUS TREES.

Of those that shed their leaves in late summer or
fall and again put out leaves in early spring, are
the hickory and pignut, the pecan: the red, black,

scrub and post oaks, maple, wild cherry, mulberry ash, persimmons and some others.

HANGING OR HAIR MOSS.

This is the moss of commerce. After being prepared, it grows on nearly all trees in the State, particularly in the south half of it. The heaviest moss is in the Hammocks and cypress swamps. It seems to grow best on the hard wood trees and cypress, but you find plenty of it on most of the pine trees, especially in the neighborhood of lakes or indeed waters of any kinds, whether lake, pond, river or springs. The higher the land the less there is of moss. I have seen moss grow on orange trees in orange groves; however where this occurs the man or party owning that grove had better sell to some man who will take care of the grove and keep the moss off the trees, for if he does not, he will in a short time find out that kind of a grove is not profitable. The moss does not grow on the body or trunk of the trees, but attaches itself to the limbs or boughs and seems to thrive best when it gets a hold near the top of the trees; it seems to feed on the air. It certainly is an air plant, for it will grow on a dead tree just as well as on a live one. It does not seem to injure any kind of trees except fruit trees, and the trouble here seems to be that the moss being so thick excludes the air partially from the fruit. The moss is attached to the limbs of the trees seemingly by very small fibrous roots which adhere very closely. It grows in bunches something like a horses tail, and hangs the same way. Some of these bunches are as much as fifty feet in length, and there may be from twenty to five hundred of these bunches hanging on one tree, varying in length from three to fifty feet; the color of them when growing is of a dark-ish gray. It bears a tiny whitish flower and blossoms for several months in the year. There is millions of tons of this moss in Florida. It is not fit for use; when taken from the trees, it seems to be of the nature of flax; it must undergo a rotting process, after which it is milled or broken, the fibre is then separated and packed in bales; it is then the moss of commerce and ready for use. It seems to the writer that right here in this moss business, there is a good opening to make money and do it legitimately and in a business way. All the moss that is prepared, and being prepared, is done in a primitive way, and nearly all by manual labor and much of it is roughly and carelessly put up with a great deal of dirt in it. It certainly would pay to form a company on a large scale, put up proper machinery at suitable places, and prepare this moss in a clear and proper way for the market and I will here venture the guess that in the near future, such a company will be organized, machinery built and much money made by it.

AIR PLANTS.

Air plants are rather singular in their nature or rather they have a peculiar penchant for fastening or growing on almost anything, whether it has roots or not; the most singular to my mind is the mistletoe. This is a mixture between the bramble bush and a vine. It seems to come by a kind of chance. (if such a thing can be) and attaches itself to some tree of the oak family, either live or deciduous and grows in a solid bunch from the size of a crows nest (which it somewhat resembles) to many feet in diameter. It usually assumes a roundish form. It is an evergreen and when found on deciduous trees. it presents a very singular appearance. when the leaves of the trees have fallen off.

There is another very singular air plant. the name of which I could not learn. In form and appearance. it is almost identical with the pine apple. It grows to a large size and produces a spike or stem, but instead of forming a solid fruit on top as does the pine apple, it separates into many bunches or forks at the top of the stem, and produces beautiful flowers of various colors, but neither fruit or seed that I could discover or find out. This plant attaches itself to almost any kind of tree, but seems more abundant on live oak in the low lands. They do grow and thrive on dead trees. and I have seen them growing on posts and against the sides of old houses and stables. There are many other varieties of these (so-called) air plants that grow here, a description of which would be very nearly a repetition of what has been above written.

. CACTUS OR COWLEEKS

The cactus family in Florida is not large. but what are here grow to an enormous size. They increase in size from year to year and produce very nice flowers until finally a freeze kills them, root and branch.

SUGAR CANE.

Sugar cane seed is not seed at all, but simply the cane stock cut in proper lengths, laid in the furrow or ground, covered entirely up : if the stocks are ripe and in good condition, they sprout at the joints and thus produce the new cane.

As a general crop in Florida, it has only been a partial success , and that only in special localities. notwithstanding, the reclaimed marsh lands is the right kind of land to raise this crop on, and when once the people get properly in the way of raising cane. in my judgement it certainly will, and must be a success. As yet sugar making in Florida is nearly all prospective ; all they can now grow is nearly all made into syrup and the most of that is consumed within her borders. Some of the syrup made in Florida is equal to the best New Orleans molasses and there is no good reason why it should not all be of a good quality, if proper machinery was put up and proper care taken in manufacturing of the syrup.

The cane seed or pieces of stocks are planted in rows several feat apart and in the rows about like corn. It is cultivated about like corn. The first season, a field or patch of cane looks very much like a field of corn ; the stocks are jointed, and the blades all resemble corn. The stocks in rich marsh lands grow as much as twenty feet high, and many of them are as much as two and a half and three inches in diameter at the butt and they carry their thickness for from six to ten feet before beginning to taper. At the proper time they tassel out something like sorgham or broom corn ; very soon ofter tasseling, they are what is called ripe, and then syrup or sugar making begins, the cane being cut and cured can be worked up months afterward. As soon as the cane is cut the roots rattoon stool out, thus producing the start for another crop, and when freezing does not interfere one planting will answer for several years and it is said that more and better sugar and syrup can be made from these rattoons or suckers the second, third, and even up to the fifth year, provided the rattoons or suckers are not allowed to cover the ground too thickly, and are not frozen. It is said by those who ought to know, that sugar cane will not ripen seed anywhere in the United States, consequently when new cane farms are first started the seed must first come from cuba or elsewhere. One thing I do know, that the parties who are now starting sugar farms in the reclaimed marsh lands of the Disston Company, imported their cane seed from Cuba. Sugar making in Florida may or may not be a success, the future alone will tell, and for the information of those who have been otherwise informed, I will only say, that while sugar has been made in Florida, it is by no means established that the business can be made a paying business.

HORSES.

The native horses are all small and of the pony order; there are, however, some very fine horses here, nearly all of which have been imported or brought here from other States and cost big money.

MULES

Are used for drawing loads, plowing, etc. They are as a general thing, brought here from Kentucky, and it is a very indifferent one that will not sell for one hundred and fifty dollars, and some good ones will bring nearly double that amount of money.

CATTLE.

The native cattle are very small and of the commonest kind, generally weighing when fat enough for beef (when they are three or fours years old) from two to three hundred pounds net, and thousands of them will not weigh that much each when hung in the market. A cow (all cattle are called cows here, no matter whether it is a bull, cow, heifer, steer, stag or calf) that will dress from two hundred and fifty to three hundred pounds of clean meat, is considered extra large. There are, however, some very fine milk cows in the State, which have been imported from other places. This kind of stock does not do very well here, either on account of climate or some other cause. It requires great care to acclimate them and even with all the care that can be taken, a large percentage of them die the first year after being brought here.

OXEN, (COWS)

Are much used for carrying, (drawing.) Remember in this country nearly everything is carried as for instance carry the cows to water, carry the log to the mill, etc.. Hauling or drawing in this country is always called carrying and anything that is small and can be carried by hand, is here called toting, as for example, tote these eggs to market, or tote this wood into the kitchen, etc. The reader will have to pardon this digression, I started on oxen, (cow). Drawing cattle may be steers, bulls or cows, and it is no unusual sight to see a bull and a cow under the same yoke, drawing a load. Cows are also driven single in shafts. You see Florida buggies drawn by a single cow. A Florida buggy is a kind of a cart mounted on two wheels with two poles for shafts, the motive power being a cow. I have seen in or on one of these vehicles, a man, a woman and five children and they seemed to be about as happy as mortals generally are, but to me it seemed rather a sorry looking crowd. I have seen as many as six and eight pairs of these cows attached, or hitched to a wagon loaded with a load that any two good

Northern horses would have walked right along with it on a good Northern road, but what the horses would, or could have done in a Florida sand road, the writer has no means of knowing.

SHEEP.

There are very few of them in the State. I kow of no reason why they should not do well.

GOATS.

This certainly would be a grand country for goats, if rough garbage and weeds are the stuff for them to forage on, and if they could be utilized in any way. As it is, very few goats are here and I do not know of any use they are being put to, except as playthings for the boys.

HOGS,

The native hogs are very small and of the razor back or cat fish variety; about one-third of the whole hog is head, then gently tapering to the tail. It takes a big hog here, when fat to weigh one hundred pounds, I mean a native Florida hog. There are some imported stock that is much better. To my mind Florida is not much of a country to raise hogs in—nothing to feed them on.

DOGS.

Of all the States that I have ever been in, Florida beats them all for mongrel curs.

CATS.

House cats are not plenty, but pole cats *are*.

CHICKENS.

Chickens do well. They are not subject to disease, and with a little proper attention, are a source of revenue. The common dunghill or mixed breed seems to be the best adapted to this climate. Nearly ever person who have tried the pure bloods or the so-called fancy chickens have failed for some cause. I can see no reason why any kind of chickens should not do well in Florida, as above stated they are not subject to any of the diseases that chickens are in the North. It is true, however, that the mites (chicken lice) are very much worse here than they are in the North, but they are easily kept down if understood. It is said, but I have not seen them, that there is a kind of a chicken flea in some parts of the State, that when these fleas get on a chicken that they become so numerous that they destroy the skin of the chicken and cause their death.

There are so many beetles, bugs, grasshoppers, crickets, and so many and various insects here during the greater part of the year, that fowls running at large about pick up their own living, and about all you have to do is feed them a little each morning and evening, shut them up at night and keep them shut up in the morning until after they lay, thus securing the eggs, then let them run the balance of the day. It is no trouble at all to raise young chickens, and it seems strange that so few are raised. They always command a good price, and eggs are never less than twenty-five cents a dozen any place in the State that I have been, and very often are sold for fifty cents a dozen, the fact is in many places fresh eggs cannot be had at any price half the time.

TURKEYS.

Turkeys for some cause that the writer does not know, seem to not do well.

DUCKS AND GEESE.

These, if properly taken care of, the right kind of coops and pens made so as to protect them from alligators, skunks and opossums, certainly ought to, and would do well, but I do not now remember of seeing a tame duck or goose in the State.

NOTE.—Since writing the above, I saw one old tame goose.

GAME.

In the Southern part of the State, deer and bears are plenty; wild turkeys, quail, and rabbits are found in nearly all parts of the State. There are a good many wild cats, and in the extreme south are found many American panthers, cougar or cata-mount, coons, opossums, and others are here in places very abundant. Squirrels are said to be plenty, but I have seen none in the State. There is abundant room and plenty of glorious fun for the sportsman and hunter, even without the squirrels, indeed you would hardly think of them when you had such game as deer and the others named, and last but not least by any means is shooting alli-gators, this in itself, is royal fun or sport; then you have wild ducks and geese, which, in season and places, are very plenty ; then there are thousands of cranes. plume birds, herrons, blue, gray and white Cormorants, black ducks, water turkeys and thousands of other birds, so that the sportsman can enjoy himself to his hearts content. A great many of the large birds known in Florida, are not seen in the North at all in a wild state.

BUZZARDS.

Buzzards are the natural scavengers of the country. They are very plenty and are especially protected by law under a severe penalty. They clean up everything of a meat or fish nature that that is thrown out, even before it becomes offensive They are so tame that they will come into your lot and even to your door, and very often you can go near enough to touch them. They are perfectly harmless and destroy nothing that is useful. It is rather a singular sight to see buzzards stepping around among your flock of chickens, (this the writer has seen many times), neither seeming to care for, or be afraid of the other.

PAROKEETS.

This is a bird of beautiful plumage. They are a kind of parrot, and it is said that when taken very young, they can be taught to imitate the human voice, and even articulate certain words. This may be so, I however have the first one yet to see or hear that made any sound, that had the faintest resemblance to the human voice to my ear.

BEES.

Both the black and Italian bees are in Florida in
a wild state; when put into hives they make or
gather some honey, but are not very profitable.
In the spring or early summer when the orange
and magnolia trees are in bloom, they do well and
gather vast quantities of honey, provided there is
not much rain. The honey plants and flowers
here, are no better than they are in the North, and
many of the best honey plants of the North are not
here at all, such as white clover, catnip, buckwheat, and others; the locust and apple are also
missing, but to balance this, Florida has the orange
and magnolia, and in the extreme South the mangrove. The bees here have a much longer season
to work in and all things being favorable, a good
colony will gather more honey here in a year than
they will farther North or where the seasons are
shorter. Bees do not seem to care to work when
the thermometer is much below sixty-five, consequently there is quite a while in the winter season
that they cannot, or do not gather honey, and if
they could, or were disposed to gather at this season, there is verry little, if any to gather. It is true
there are many varieties of flowers in full bloom in
mid-winter, but there is no honey at all in most of
them, and such as do have honey in them, is so
shaped that the bees cannot get it. Again it is
never so cold here but what the bees are active in
the'r hives, and they have brood at all seasons of

the year, and when they cannot gather honey from outside, they consume what is inside. It is said that bees do much better further south, especially so in the mangrove country. From my own observation, if I were to raise bees I would seek other quarters to operate in.

SNAKES.

Rattlesnakes, of which there are several kinds or species—Moccasin and Cottonmouth, seem to be the most dangerous. These all have fangs and their bite is frequently fatal, unless the proper remedies are at hand to apply. I have seen the skins of Rattlesnakes in Florida that were all of twelve feet in length and to all appearance the snake when living must have been eight inches in diameter in the thickest part. This kind however are not very plenty. There is a rattlesnake called the Ground Rattler, that is plenty and perhaps the most dangerous of all the snakes of Florida because of his habits. This ground rattle snake is small; never exceeds a couple of feet in length; is of a kind of grayish color; he crawls under pieces of bark, wood or boards; coils himself up there and should you go to remove the matter with which he is covered, or step on the same, you are almost certain to be bitten. This snake gives no warning, although he has rattles he does not use them only in the act of biting, the warning is then too late. Not so with his big brother, which always warns before biting, and unless you can come upon them very suddenly there is not much danger from the larger species, for there is generally enough time between the warning and the bite for you to get out of their way and I would here advise you not to tackle (attempt to kill) one of these big fellows unless you are well prepared to do battle or have a good rifle with you. Then besides these two species above named, there is a medium sized rattle snake that presents very nearly the same appearance as the large one, whose habits are about the same. It is said that this is a distinct species I did not investigate this snake business very closely. but from what I saw and know of this snake, I am of the opinion that when he lives as long as his big brother, he will be about the same size.

As for the Moccasin snake, I have never seen one, although they are said to be numerous and their bite very poisonous. The most danger from them is that they lie out at night on the public roads, foot paths and even on board walks and if you should happen to step or tramp on one of them you are almost certain to be bitten.

The cotton mouth is a kind of adder something like what the Northern people call a blowing viper When disturbed they throw back the upper part of their neck. thus exposing the entire inside of their mouth, which very much resembles an open ball of cotton, hence the name cotton mouth. It is said this snake is not apt to bite unless provoked or suddenly surprised.

There are many, very many other kinds and species of snakes in Florida, as the black snake, a large gray snake, coach whip, (Northern people call it black racer), garter house and others, none of which are very dangerous.

SALAMANDERS AND CHAMELEONS.

These are a species of lizzards from four to eight inches long; they burrow in the sand, throwing up great piles of it, especially in the scrub pine lands, you will frequently find thousands of these little sand hills about the size of a half bushel on a single acre of land. You do not want much of that kind of land to raise oranges or truck on.

GOPHERS.

Gophers are a kind of rat or ground mole that burrows in the ground and a half a dozen of them will destroy a young orange grove by eating off the roots in a very short time it only left alone. The only way to stop them is to trap them, (which is very hard to do) or dig after until you catch them, which is quite an undertaking, as they get away about as fast as you get after them.

COOTERS.

This is a kind of terrapin or land turtle, which also burrows in the sand. They are harmless as far as I can ascertain. When they are full grown they weigh about twenty pounds and are said to be very good to eat, equally as much so as soft shell turtles, of which there are abundance in many of the lakes in Florida.

MOSQUITOS, GALINIPPERS,

And Gnats are very numerous and very pestiferous. You hear it said and read it in newspapers published here, that there are some mosquitos in Florida, but in many places they are comparatively free from them. No person does say that there are none here, and no person can truthfully say but what they are very abundant all over the State· In one of the towns that is said to be free from these pests, you cannot walk the streets or sit in the house five minutes without having the pests singing about your ears, and it is impossible to sleep at night without being protected by a good mosquito bar, and the bar must be tucked under the mattress and perfectly tight or they will find you under it. If they only lasted a short time you could stand it, but they pest you for nearly nine months of the year. This is almost too long, even for all the advantages Florida promises to give: then the black gnats are no pleasant companions, they get into your mouth, eyes and nose and while they do not present their bills with as much pertinacity as do their big brothers, (the mosquitos and galinippers), and while they do not trouble you in the dark or while trying to sleep, they are very unpleasant to have about: then in connection with the mosquitos and galinippers and gnats, you have the

FLEAS

Innumerable Cimex Lecturlarius. The per-

fume from these latter when you smash one of them
is indeed very different from "attar of roses," and
they are very numerous and can be found inside
and out of about all the houses in Florida, whether
inhabited or otherwise. The winged insects and
bugs are so numerous that it is almost impossible
to read or do anything in the house after dark by
candle light without shutting doors and windows
tightly, or having very fine screens over them,
hence in traveling through Florida by rail after
night, you will see large fires built near the dwelling houses. You wonder what these fires are for
in the warm weather. Here is the secret; to destroy the bugs and insects, which it does to a certain extent, but the mosquito cannot be caught in
that way: he is a night bird to a very great extent
and keeps away from the fire. The only way to
dispose of them effectually is to catch him, which
requires about the same amount of exertion and
dexterity that it does to catch a flea, and after you
have him, squeeze him gently between your thumb
and finger until he is dead. If these pests named
were all, you still might put up with all of them,
for the seeming advantages to be derived, but when
the "red bugs," and sand fleas begin to levy tribute
you will begin to think Florida has some pests.

RED BUGS AND JIGGERS.

Red bugs and jiggers are all over the State, in
fields and forests, in the sand, in the grass, on flowers and weeds, on the trees and bushes and particu-

larly on old logs and in the moss that grows on
the trees. They, however, do not infest the houses
but it is almost impossible to keep them off your
body; they are so small that you can scarcely see
them with the naked eye, but when they get on
you, as they certainly will, if you walk around
much or stand among the grass or weeds. The
first intimation you have of them being on you, is
an itchiness, which you will naturally rub or
scratch, which, instead of relieving, only increases
the irritation, and the more you rub or scratch the
itchier the place becomes; on the first opportunity,
you make an examination, you will then discover
the skin is red and inflamed—the bugs are there
sure enough! and at work, and unless you get them
killed very soon, the place where they are becomes very sore and begins to slough (sluff) off.
The best remedy known is to rub with kerosene,
(common coal oil); very strong spirits of camphor
will also answer; as soon as you discover that the
bugs are on you, if one application does not kill
them, the second will be sure death. To avoid
getting the bugs on you either stay in the house,
or rub your body all over with coil oil before dressing in the morning, then you can go where you
please with impunity. So far as red bugs and jiggers are concerned, there is another pest that you
will likely become acquainted with before you are
very long in the "Land of Sunshine and flowers:"
it is the

WOOD TICK.

These, however, are not very plenty; they get on your body and may be on for days before you know it; they, like the red bug, produce an itchiness; in trying to relieve, which you will find a small lump or protuberance, on close inspection you will find the tick about the size of a large sheep louse; no trouble to find or see them; you will find him securely fastened. The head of the tick is formed something like the sharp point of a wood screw with the thread cut the reverse way and unless you unscrew the tick and get it all out of the place where it was fastened, will become very sore Many persons not knowing the nature of this pest, seize hold of the body of the tick and pull them off; in that case you almost invariably let the head part remain in your flesh which naturally must beal out. I have named some of the most pestiferous pests. There are plenty of others that you will become acquainted with should you at any time spend a year in Florida.

BUGS, BEETLES. &C.

These are here by the thousands of millions. The vast majority of them, as far as I know, are harmless, and are useful for chicken feed, if for nothing else.

ROACHES.

Roaches are very numerous and are, or do destroy some things when they get into the houses, as they generally do and not in small quantities either. I have seen roaches in Florida one and one-half inches long and fully five-eighths of an inch wide.

COMMON OR HOUSE FLIES.

These need no particular description as they are common all over the world in certain seasons of the year. In Florida we have them in abundance during the whole year.

MICE.

Mice are plentiful and just as destructive as they are in the North, and seem to be about the same kind of mice.

RATS.

I have not seen or heard of a black or gray rat in the State. I have no doubt they are here, notwithstanding, there is an Albino or large white rat here domesticated, and they are used as cats for catching mice.

TOADS AND FROGS.

These are numerous here, and the only difference I see is they are smaller. There is a kind of toad here that makes a noise very much like a duck and there is a cricket that hollars just like a young chicken.

SOMETHING ABOUT THE STATE AT LARGE AND SOME OTHER THINGS.

The area of the State is about 60,000 square miles, or say 38,400.000 acres. Fully the one-half is covered with water and swamps, about one-half of the balance is marsh and low, flat land, two-thirds of which can never be utilized for any purpose; this leaves about one-sixth of the State that is upland. Now perhaps one-half of this, or one-twelfth of the State, which can with proper drainage, good cultivation and abundance of fertilizer, be made to produce vegetables and almost anything that will grow in a semi-tropical climate.

As to cost of production and what they will bring in cash, will perhaps be the subject of another chapter in this or some other book. If it were not that many of the products of Florida are raised and marketed in a season of the year that they bring extra good prices, the producer would have very little but his labor for his pains, as it is, if the producer had to entirely depend upon the products of the soil for a living, many of them would have very short rations or allowance.

About now you will ask, what then are the attractions and inducements for people to go to Florida? The answer may be given by asking this question: "What are the attractions and inducement for people to go to Saratoga Springs, Catskill and White mountains, or any and all of the famous summer resorts in the North?" Very few people go there, or to any of those places with a view to make money, (except the hotel keepers), but rather for recreation and rest. This is all well enough and perfectly legitimate when you have ample means and can afford it. Now, these sum-

mer resorts are generally so situated and their locations are such, that there is not much chance for
sharpers and speculators, consequently you do not
find many of this character there. Now Florida is
a natural winter resort for the class of people who
have leisure and money to spend, and who wish to
avoid the long cold winters of the North, and the
Territory being larger; selections of place and locality can be made to suit the purses of all. The
winters here are almost like summer in the North,
and for some three or four months there are comparatively few pests to trouble you. For rest and
recreation, this State cannot be surpassed in the
Union, and I doubt if in the known world, but
when that is said, it is nearly all that can be truthfully said about it, but the chances for speculation
here are too great to be overlooked; many places
of beauty, must be and are improved; large hotels
and boarding houses are built, and paper towns
are laid out, number of inhabitants are kind of
miraculously increased, flaming circulars are sent
broadcast over the North. These circulars as a
general thing contain some truth, and they are so
worded and prepared that they seem to describe
the country almost as being a paradise—all the
good is told and well told, and the bad is kept in
the background and is seldom, if ever mentioned.

Syndicates or companies of speculators are formed a few thousand acres are bought, the land costing
from one dollar and twenty-five cents to three and

a half dollars per acre, a town plot or winter resort
is laid off; certain lots are always reserved for
churches and schools; a good deal of money is
spent in advertising and a little in cutting streets
and roads in the new city; a little bit of a shanty is
put up and advertised as a grand hotel. There is
usually a cut or picture on the advertisement or
circular showing a magnificent hotel with carriage
in waiting to take you to and from the depot, also
showing magnolia and palmetto and orange trees
laden with fruit. This all looks splendid on paper
when the facts are, that in many cases there is not
a magnolia or palmetto tree, or a bearing orange
tree within many miles ot this particular locality,
and the hotel is as above described, this, however,
is called BOOMING. These circulars also set forth
that there are about so many inhabitants there now
and for a short time small lots, say 40x100 feet,
can be had for from two to ten dollars. each. but
you must be in a hurry about it for the lots are
going off (selling) very rapidly and the price will
be double or more in a short time. You are also
told that this land is first quality, and on it can be
raised all kinds of vegetables, tropical and semi-
tropical fruit, and strawberries—no end to them,
and for a very small sum you can build you a
house to live in; some of them even say that for
so much, they will put up for you a neat cottage
and have it ready so that all you have to do is to
come right along, (better not come right away, the

house may not be ready for some time). Many of
them tell you that it is just as pleasant to live in
Florida in the summer as it is in witner. This all
looks splendid on paper, and it does not, according
to these circulars, seem to require much capital to
own a house and lot in Florida. About the next
thing you begin to talk of this matter to your neighbors and they become interested and in short
among you, you have sent the syndicate or company a few hundred dollars, in due course of time
you get your deeds for the land or lots; this is all
bona fide and in proper shape; your title is good
and the land or lots are there sure enough, and
you are a land owner in Florida and it has not cost
you a great deal either. But now let us figure a
little and see if some person has not paid pretty
well for the whistle, considering its size. Suppose
you pay only five dollars for a lot 40x100 feet, you
get four thousand square feet of land, this land cost
the company, say two dollars per acre and perhaps
two dollars more an acre to advertise and getting
you to buy. Now we find that there is a little over
ten such lots in an acre, so you see you have paid
the company at the rate of over fifty dollars for
what cost them not over four dollars, now this is
quite a neat little job, a clear profit of not less than
forty-five dollars on an investment of four dollars.
Very often after the company have sold the majority of their lots they abandon the enterprise alto-
gether; they have accomplished their object to

make money ; they have made their pile, (so to speak) and while they have failed to do as their circulars represented, what they have done has been within the statute and there you are and without remedy ; the enterprise is a fizzle or failure ; to be a little more explicit, it is a fraud and a swindle The only thing you can do is to bear your loss and look out and not buy the next time until you see what you are getting. This is no fancy picture nor is there any imagination about it. Such cases are constantly occurring and can easily be specified. I would not have the reader understand that all land, speculations and enterprises in Florida are of this character, but I would have you understand that they will all bear watching, and some of them very closely, and I here and now advise you to hold on to your money until you have thoroughly investigated the case, and as for me, I would not entrust this investigation to any one, but before I invested a single dollar. I would go and see for myself. There are certainly many good chances to speculate, and make money rapidly in Florida, but in order to do it, you must be right here on the ground with the money to take advantage of the chances as they occur. What a man wants to make money here, is some capital, the more the better, fair judgement and some pluck, (vim), but unless a person has some considerable cash on hand, there are very many places preferable to Florida to live in or make money.

COPY OF LETTER.

" ED. FALCON :—Never having written you since my arrival in "the Land of Sunshine and Flowers," I thought the views and ideas of one who now lives here would not be uninteresting to some of your readers, for some of them, like the writer, may be foolish enough to want to exchange the certainties of old Albemarle for the very uncertainties of the very great humbuggers of this very great myth cf the land of gnats, sand flies, sand, i.e. Florida. I have been in this State just nine months and can truly say that the only ones that I have seen, who like it, are those who came down several years ago and happened to strike land that was then of comparatively no value, and which has since risen to value on account of immigration or those who come here with thousands of dollars in their pockets, and speculate in lands and town lot sat almost fabulous prices. I myself came here with a few hundred dollars in my pockets with the idea in my head that I had only to invest that in either merchandise or a piece of land, to live ever after in ease and comfort. I was wrong, my ideas were based on the articles of which the State is composed, namely sand. I found I could not buy a building lot anywhere convenient to the business portion of the town (Orlando) without expending the whole of the little cash I had brought with me in the naked lot alone. It is true I can buy a small lot 50x140 feet about one mile from the centre of the town for two hundred dollars in cash down, but why are these lots sold so cheaply? I will tell. Hold your ear close that I may whisper it, for I must not speak of these things aloud. It is because the lands are so low that they are almost entirely cover-ed with water and a person cannot walk upon the streets where they are located, unless he has on what our fisher-man in North Carolina ca l hip boots. These are facts and yet they sell lots. Why? I will tell you in the fall and winter when they are comparatively dry, the Northern man with capital in his pocket comes down to invest, he is taken hold of by the land sharps, (real estate agents)—no reflection Mr. Editor, and first shown higher up town, which does not overflow, and offers them at from eight hundred to two thousand dollars per lot: of course when he is offered the other at two hundred dollars because they are a little farther out; (nothing said about their being low); he nabs them at once, goes to work and puts a shell on them, costing from two to six hundred dollars and rents them out at from twelve to twenty dollars a month—the same house with 50x100 feet that rents in Elizabeth City for six dollars a month would rent here quickly for from twenty to twenty-five dollars per month

Trade in merchandising is now very dull here, but the town authorities are using their best endeavors to make times brisker by putting on new takes. We have a water closet tax at the rate of thirteen dollars per year, which the poor renter has to pay; a little street tax of six dollars per year for each voter. These are only in proportion to other taxes, which you see are all very moderate.

There is only one thing that keeps, or holds at least one-third of the population of this section here; want of means to get away; They spent their all to get here and now can't save enough of money to pay their way back home.

Talking about rents, I pay for a shell that is neither lathed, plastered or ceiled on the inside, and with boards running up and down on the outside on a lot of about seventy-five feet square; the modest little sum of fifteen dollars per month, payable in advance every time, and then under obligations to take it for the whole year. My store rent is more reasonable, being only twenty-five dollars per month for a room about nine by forty-five feet but that is really low in proportion to some others. If you ask me, can people stand this long? I will answer no! Business here will not justify it and I will answer that before the summer is over, many will be compelled to sell out and close up.

You never see corn growing here or any of the cereals or grass. All of the feed is imported and nearly all except a few inferior vegetables that is used here for food by the inhabitants is brought here from the North and West.

I rode out in the country on Sunday last to admire the "Land of Flowers." I only saw pine barrens, swamps and lakes, what in North Carolina would be called ponds No flowers, no fields of corn, wheat, cotton or clover, nothing in fact but barrens with now and then a field of sand with young orange trees set out in them. But they can raise cabbage, potatoes and other vegetables if they only choose to do so. I have it from the very lips of a man from Ohio, now living here. who has tried it and he says as good vegetables can be raised here as any-where in the world, and that the cost of raising them will not be much more than double the price you can sell them for. I, of course don't know whether this is true or not, but this. I do know that all with whom I have talked on the subject, say that the cost of culti-vation far exceeds the prices obtained.

This country has a great reputation for climate, in fact it is all climate and sand, flies and other pests, such as it is. I have been told that the winters here are de-lightful. I suppose it must be so since they all say so, but I can say for myself, I have not found it so. My whole family, including my wife and myself, have suf-fered more from the cold and colds here than on the bleak cost of North Carolina during the fall and winter of 1885 and 1886.

Comment on the above letter is useless. It is the experience of thousands in Florida to-day, and will be of thousands more, until people come to know the true condition of the State, its resources and drawbacks.

SOCIETY.

The state of society may be truly said to be self-ish in nearly every sense of the word. A North-ern man or woman, (when I say Northern, I mean anybody outside of Florida, whether from the North

South, East or West), on first coming to the State ;
especially if they have money, which is soon found
out by land agents and speculators, they are taken
in hand by interested parties, and carried all over
the town and surrounding country in good style,
usually with a spanking team, rigged in the latest
style, and if you are to be out all day, a good lunch
and may be something to wash it down will be
taken.   Either that or arrangements made at some
convenient place.   In either case, the trip costs
you nothing (directly).   You will always find the
driver a first-rate fellow ; he knows everybody he
meets and will introduce you and the newly made
acquaintance will give a flattering account of the
country, its beauties and advantages.   After leaving him, the driver will again take up the conversation.   After expatiating on what the man said,
he will show you that there is much more to be told
in his case   He will then perhaps give you a history of the recent acquaintance which is always
marvelous, particularly in the way that he has ac-
cumulated wealth : usually the party came to Florida very poor, either bought or took up a piece of
land, cleared it off, fenced broke up, and planted
a grove.   There it is and you can, and do see it
with your own eyes.   These trees are from seven
to ten years old and this season will have on each
tree from a thousand to five thousand oranges ;
(mighty good trees) these at a cent and a half a
piece will bring, well you can figure for yourself ;

about this time you are some place else, and another new acquaintance is made and about the
same story is gone over again perhaps with a little
variation, but always better, all the time, the
brightest of the bright side is shown and kept before you and expatiated upon in the most glowing
language and the very best and choicest places are
shown you, thus the day passes.

You turn to the starting point, another engage-
ment is made at the earnest solicitation of the party
who has carried you around for another drive in a
different direction on some other day, in the near
future you leave him for the present. You, however, scarcely get away from him until some one
else hails you. These men get to know you very
soon and promise to take you around to-morrow or
next day; you soon begin to think these people are
very clever and very sociable, and that this is certainly a very nice country to live in; thus it goes
on for a week or so until you make a purchase,
which generally reveals the true state of your finan
ces; as soon as this is known, or if you have invested about what you intended and express yourself in that way, these fellows will hardly recog-
nize you on the street, and many of the parties to
whom you have been introduced, will have forgotten you entirely; the party that sold you, (so to
speak) has accomplished his end, made his money
paid his stool pigeons and now is looking out for
other victims, while others got left, as they say

down here in Florida. Now when this transaction is thoroughly sifted, we find that by a previous arrangement that nearly all of the persons with whom you have talked and been introduced to, there is an understanding that they are to talk just about the way they did, and they always manage to have enough show of truth in the whole business to dazzle and fascinate you, (and let me here say that they understand their business) and get you to invest your money, and on further investigating you will find as you are shown around by different firms that you seldom meet any of the parties with whom you had become acquainted through other parties. Should it so happen, you are quickly drawn away from them. This being the case, and it is exactly. it is plain to be seen (not at the time but afterward) that nearly everybody is interested in land speculation either directly or indirectly, and as soon as they have your money or signature, you can row your own boat. As is often the case when notes are given and you fail to meet it, then the friendship is shown, for often the law is enforced the day the note falls due, and the laws in Florida are such that debts of all kinds can be collected at once, if at all collectable. This same stran or thread runs through all the business transactions with storekeepers, mechanics &c. So long as you can pay cash, it is all right and friends are numerous, but when short of funds and want a favor, in ninety-nine cases out of every hundred, you will stick.

This, then fully demonstrates that the society and people of Florida, as a general thing, are selfish. There are some honorable exceptions, but they only prove the rule. There are very few neighbors, all are strangers as it were, and each one is taking care of him or herself, while their way of doing business is in some respects commendable, in others it is far from honorable. The rule here is to buy and sell for cash. This is all right, but if the trade is of such a nature that money can be made out of it, they will hold out every inducement for you to buy, (not particular about the cash,) but as soon as the trade is made and closed, as a matter of business of course you give your obligations to pay at a certain time and just as soon as the time is up, if not paid the statute is put in force and the money is made, no matter how badly or who it hurts. There are a few exceptions to this, but they are very few indeed. My advice here, is never give a note or obligations of any kind in Florida, unless you are sure you know where the money is to come from to pay it, and that you are sure you will get it in time, or my word for it, you will have trouble and costs to pay also.

MISREPRESENTATION.

There are but few men or parties who are in any kind of business in Florida, but what will misrepresent, or at least make things appear to be fully as large as they are and many of them seem to think it no special harm, but rather smart to repre-

sent an article as first-class when they know it is
not, or to say an article cost so much when it did
not cost one-half of what they say.   Another thing
is very common here and that is to have several
prices for the same article, the lowest of which is
always high enough. If you happen to know
what a thing is worth. you can generally buy
about right, otherwise you will in all probability
pay double or treble for it.   This is considered all
right and counted as smart, the fact is the motto
seems to be, "get money, get it honestly if you
can, if not, get it any way, so you don't steal it and
get caught.

POLITICS.

There really does not seem to be much bother
about it in the State.   The proclivities however,
are Democratic, but you hear very little said and
elections are held with very much less clamor and
corruption than they are in the North.   The ma-
nipulating or wire working (if any) are done in
the registration of voters.   A man connot vote unless he is registered such a length of time prior to
the election, and as the Board of Registration is
located at the county seat of each county, you must
therefore go to the county seat to find out if you
are registered or not. otherwise you will find out
on election day, as the list of registered voters is
sent with the other election papers to each polling
place in the county.   As a general thing nearly all
voters, both white and black, are registered and so

far as I know or can see, or find out, each and
every man, both white and black, casts their vote
as they please without let or hindrance from any
person ; the stories you hear in the North to the
contrary notwithstanding.   I would not have the
reader understand that there is no electioneering
here about election times, for there is and sometimes excitement runs very high, but I have never
heard of any money being offered for votes in the
State, it may have been done however.

NIGGERS.

The word nigger is a term of general accepta-
tion all over the State, and it is as much used by
the blacks as the whites, and no disrespect is shown
or attended when the word is used.

There seems to be no authentic censes or account of the number or even relative number of
white and black inhabitants in the State, but it is
admitted by nearly all persons who seem to know
that the niggers in the State outnumber the whites
by very considerable.   Some of the niggers are
industrious and are doing well—in many cases
they are doing better than the whites as they stand
this hot climate better than the whites, but take
them as a class, they are lazy and worthless, and
will not work unless compelled by necessity.   Many
of them live more like brutes than human beings.
They are even (many of them) too lazy to cook
meat or mutton corn, but eat them raw.   Then on
the other hand, there are niggers who have pride

enough to take care of themselves, and who are just as respectable and live just as good as any of the whites.   On an average in doing manual labor two white men will do about as much work in a given time as six niggers would in the same time. The black mechanic will, however, do about as much work as the white one in the same length of time, and there are some very good mechanics among them.

INDIANS.

There are in the Southern part of the State, principally in Dade, Monroe and Manatee counties about five hundred Indians.   This number, like all other accounts of the inhabitants of the State are guessed at, and I guess the number is too high by nearly one-half.   Be this as it may, a remnant of the once powerful seminoles are still in Florida. They seem to be perfectly harmless and subsist by hunting, fishing and raising a few cattle.   Some of them occasionally come as far North as Kissimmee City to exchange their furs, pelts, alligator teeth, &c., for groceries, fire water, (whiskey), a little clothing, gewgaws, and ribbons.   Their clothing is very scant, nor is it in the height of fashion.   It consists of a garment made something like a short shirt, over which is usually worn a kind of jacket and head gear of some stuff or cloth usually red or other glaring, or gaudy color, trimmed with beads, alligator teeth or some gaudy tinsel.   The bucks (men) seem to care more for their head gear than

any other part of their clothing. The squaws
(women) dress about as the men, they however,
wear no head gear, but instead thereof, usually
wear moccasins. None of the bucks 'wear moccasins, except the chiefs or those in authority, who
wear in addition to the above described dress moccasins and kind of pantaloons or trowsers made of
buckskin and being adorned with a wide flap or
fringe down the legs about where the outside seam
of pants are. The principal chief has his head
gear also trimmed with eagle feathers and wears in
addition a fancy breech cloth fancifully trimmed
with tinsel and gay colors. The papoose (children) run entirely naked until they are ten or
twelve years of age over the country, everglades.
&c., living in skin tents, bark cabins, hollow trees,
etc. A large majority of them can speak enough
English to make their wants known.

MINERALS.

There is in some places in the Northern part of
the State some iron ore, but as yet not found in
paying quantities. There are no other minerals
that I know or can hear of in the State except sulphur and that only in the water. Clay Springs
are so strongly impregnated with sulphur that you
can smell it several hundred yards away from the
springs and when you approach the springs you
can see the sulphur all around the margins. Place
a half dollar in the water and in a very few minutes it turns to a yellow color, resembling gold.

It however soon turns black on exposure to the air. There are many other sulphur springs in the State. The deep down water seems to all be impregnated with sulphur. Nearly all the artesian wells produce sulphur water.

STONE COAL.

There is not any in the State that I know of.

FUEL.

Wood is the only fuel. Pine wood is usually used (the oak is very hard to chop) and while it is plenty and can be had for the gathering. The wood choppers here put up the wood in what they call strans. A stran of wood is said to be eight feet long, four feet high and wide as a stove wood stick is long. They will cut the wood whatever length you want, not exceeding twenty-four inches. A twelve inch length is the same price as a twenty-four inch length. It seems like as if the charge was for the work and not for the wood. Those strans they will deliver to you cut, split up and all ready for the stove for one dollar and fifty cents a stran, so you see after all fuel costs right smart. There is, however, the consolation that this climate, especially in the summer time, does not require much fuel. The wood is always cut from the green tree and you must have lighter wood to start your fire with. This lighter wood is from old pine trees that have fallen down and the sap or white wood has all rotted off, leaving nothing but the fat pine heart and old pine knots. Lighter wood in Florida is called kindling wood in the North. This lighter wood is delivered to you in chunks and costs about two dollars a stran and you must split it up into kindling yourself or get it done; you can suit yourself about this.

HAULING OR CARRYING.

You seldom hear the word haul or hauling in the sense used by Northern people. If they haul anything here, it is called carrying. They carry a stran of wood, they carry the lumber for a house from the mill, they carry the stock to water, in fact any and everything that is transported on wagons, drawn by horses, mules or oxen or that is driven before you is carried and any and everything that is carried or transported by hand in this country is toted, so it is tote me a pail of water, tote me some wood or tote these eggs to the store, or this satchel to the depot, &c. Many other strange and singular terms are used, both by whites and blacks, such as "sure enough." This expression is used when anything startling is related as for example: John Smith's house was burned last night. The person to whom it is related will invariably exclaim "sure enough," and I do not know but that the expression is about as elegant as the Northern people do, "is that so?" Again, "done gone" is another common expression. Ask if a man has done a certain work, and if he has, the answer will be, "Yes, he done gone and did it," or did such a person go west? "Yes, he done gone last week. Again "that away"

instead of that or this way, always putting the "a"
before the "way," and many more seemingly ab-
surd expressions, which no doubt originated among
the niggers, but are now used indiscriminately
with the whites and blacks ; there are exceptions,
but they are few and far between, and strange to
say people from the North fall right in and use
these same expressions quite soon after coming
here,

DWELLING HOUSES.

Dwelling houses are mainly built of wood (yellow pine) and are covered with cypress shingles,
tin or boards ; the foundation is live oak blocks
when obtainable, otherwise pine blocks. These
blocks are pieces cut off trees from two to six feet
long, according as you want your house elevated,
and are set on end on top of the ground (sand) for
the top is the solid part of the country ; these blocks
are from a foot to two feet in diameter, these being
placed in position the structure is then built. A
common house or shell is made of light timber
usually two by four inch stuff, enclosed with plank
(inch boards) running up and down, sometimes
stripped and very often not, a single story about
eight feet high, the inside divided into two apart-
ments, however usually all in one ; the roof may
be plank, shingles or tin, according to the means
of the builder, it is a fact that there is not one roof
in ten in Florida that turns water perfectly, no

matter of what kind of material the roof is composed. The common houses have no inside finish
whatever. This kind of a house can be built cheaply ; the lumber will cost delivered on the ground
about thirteen dollars per thousand feet, so for
about fifty or seventy-five dollars you can have a
house of your own and then sit down under your
own roof and contemplate on your surroundings,
and thus enjoy this splendid country, composed of
climate, sand and some other things, but a better class of houses are built about as follows :
Foundation about as above described. then a regular frame (balloon) is made of heavier timber,
novelty siding is used, planed and matched flooring is put in, a good shingle or tin root is put on,
doors and windows are put in places, the inside
divided into rooms, &c., outside painted, then it is
ready to occupy if the party has means ; the inside
may be ceiled with plank or lathed and plastered,
chimneys and fire places put in and fixed up and
furnished as you may desire, this, then is called a
a very good house in Florida. Such a house will
cost from four hundred to four thousand dollars,
depending on just two things alone and these are
the size of the house and the size of your money
pile, then there are a few extra good houses built
here of both wood and brick. They do have brick
in Florida, but they are nearly all made and burned at Atlanta, Georgia. They cost in Florida from
leven to sixteen dollars per thousand, yet there

are some brick houses built in the Southern part of
the State, and quite a good many in the Northern
part. This is just about the size of it. You can
build just the kind of a house you may want in
Florida as well as anywhere else, provided you
have the money to do it with. I know of houses
being built here that cost from fifteen to twenty
thousand dollars. The material out of which they
were built was all shipped from the North. These
kind of houses are generally put up by parties who
have a big lot of land. A new town or orange
groves for sale is not always the case, but when
you find a party making a big show of this or
any other sort in Florida, it will be well enough to
keep an eye to windward.

As above stated nearly all the brick used in
Florida are taken there from Atlanta, Georgia.
There are several places in the State that brick
are made. They, however, are very inferior on
account of being too much sand in the clay, or
the sand not having enough of clay in it, anyhow
the brick are worthless. It is claimed that a party
has recently made a discovery and I believe has it
patented, that by a certain process they can make
a kind of brick or artificial stone out of this Florida
sand. They put up the sand in blocks about the
size of ordinary brick and without burning. They
harden these blocks so that they do not crumble
and they are just about as strong as well burned
brick The claim is that they will stand fire and

are no more subject to crumble from exposure to the weather than good brick. I have seen some of these blocks and to all appearance the discovery seems to be a good one. This party claims they can furnish these sand bricks or blocks at from six to eight dollars a thousand—a thousand of them will build about as much wall as twelve hundred common bricks. They further claim when the right kind of mortar or cement is used that the entire wall becomes solid; they further claim they can make door sills, lintels, cornice, mouldings, etc., right out of the sand. Should this prove a success, it will to a great extent, revolutionize the building of houses in Florida and some other places as well. This, however, to a very great extent is prospective, like a great many other things here. The worst feature about building here, is that the lumber is all worked green. A log is thrown on the mill at one end and comes off at the other end in the shape of flooring, siding, moulding, etc., as the case may be, or rough boards or dimension lumber, and is taking at once and put into buildings. Very many times trees that were standing in the morning, in the evening of that same day are built in dwellings, thus you see building houses entirely of the greenest kind of lumber; this being the case the lumber seasons in the building and naturally gives away, leaving cracks and open places, making bad work. The lumber is of such a nature that if to season before using, unless very

carefully stacked, it warps and twists all out of
shape and becomes so hard that it is almost impossible to work it to any advantage or satisfaction,
as it breaks and splits very easily. When green,
it is soft and pliable and easily worked and bent in
almost any shape you may want it, but when dry
it is stiff, hard and will not, and cannot be made
to assume any shape, but that to which it has
dried.

Yellow pine is the only kind of native lumber
that is used for building purposes, except cypress,
which is too expensive on account of the difficulty
of getting it out of the swamps, otherwise it would
take the place of white pine in the North, of which
its nature partakes, in that it is soft, straight in the
grain and does not warp or twist in drying or seas-
oning. Magnolia trees make good lumber, but it
is too scarce to amount to anything. The live, and
other oaks when sawed, assume all kinds of shapes
consequently are of no account only for blocks for
foundations.

WELLS OF WATER.

There is no trouble to sink a well anywhere in
Florida, all you have to do is to dig a hole in the
sand big enough so that you can work in it. After
you get down several feet, a box three or four feet
square without a bottom or top must be placed in
the hole with a stout piece of scantling in each
corner inside; these pieces of timber should be
from sixteen to twenty feet in length—of course the

upper end sticks away above the hole; this timber
is to nail your boards to, to increase the height of
your box. now put on a few pieces of boards so as
to bring your box on a level with the surface of the
land, then get inside and throw out some more
sand; as fast as you throw out the sand from below
the box will sink, thus keeping your well walled
or curbed; when you have gone down a foot or
so, better climb out and put more boards on your
timbers or the sand will come in over the top of
what is on, soon you will strike the surface water;
this you must go through for it is fit for nothing,
continue until you strike hard pans; this has been
described. You must go through this and as soon
as you strike water below the hard pan, it is said
to be good and wholesome. Your trouble now is
to keep the surface water outside of your box or
curbing. This so-called good water is found at
different depths, say from ten to thirty feet from
the surface, depends if the land is high or low; in
any and all cases, your box or curbing must reach
from the top to the bottom of the well or the sand
will run in and fill it up, thus after having dug this
hole or well to the proper depth and curbed it, the
water settles into it sometimes to the depth of several feet, and very often fills up above the hard pan :
when this is the case, you must pump or draw it
out—it may be several times. at least until it becomes clear, you can then use it, in fact you will
be obliged to use it, simply because you can get no

other. The only other remedy is to procure a tank and catch rain water, which, without ice is not much better. While many of the lakes, streams and springs and some of the wells in Florida seem to have nice, clear, pellucid water in them. I have never had a good drink of water since I entered the State. The water is all warm, insipid and of a brackish taste and the deeper the well, the warm· er the water, and if it were not that ice can be had at almost all the principal towns and cities at reas* onable prices, say fifty cents per hundred pounds wholesale, that is by agreeing to take from one to three hundred pounds per day. At retail, that is from five to ten pounds per day, or a chunk now and then, the price is from one to five cents per pound. This ice is all made by machinery run by steam. The ice is made somewhat on the princi* ciple of making ice cream: the water to be frozen, is placed in square cans of the size of which the cake of ice is intended to be when frozen. These cans are placed in a large metal or wooden tank or vat, each can or mould being held in position by a frame or kind of wicker work. the tank is then filled with a freezing liquid or brine. There is another receptacle or tank in which is some kind of chemicals, which is called the charge. This is so arranged with pipes and connections running through and about the brine, surrounding the cans or ice moulds, that the whole business is set in motion by machinery driven by an engine that they turn out solid cakes of ice about every twenty-four hours. The capacity of these machines are from a few hundred pounds to many tons of ice per day, and their cost from about eight hundred to fifty thousand dollars, according to their capacity. There is said to be a small machine intended for family use, and driven by hand power, the capacity of which is fifteen pounds per hour and the cost of which is only about twenty-five dollars. I have not seen any of these machines, therefore cannot vouch for the truth of the report, if, however it be true, there surely is no reason why each family should not have the luxury.

TAXES.

The method of assessing or laying taxes in Florida are rather loose and appears novel to a Northern man. There is but one assessor for each county. He advertises to be in the different election districts on certain days—I believe two days each year, at a designated place in the district—usually at the voting place, each voter and property holder of personal or real estate, must report to him on one of these days all of his possessions, both personal and real, and he is provided with printed forms or blanks. If you own any lands or lots, you must give him the description and number of the same, also the township and range, block and numbers of lots, as the case may be, all of which is a matter of record at the county seat. You are then required to fix a price on ev-

erything you have or own, down to your household
goods, and certify over your signature to the truth
of the same. All voters under fifty years of age
in addition to the above, have to pay a poll tax of
six dollars a year. This, I believe is applied to
fixing and making roads and streets; the other
general taxes, that is State and county, are from
one and a half to two per cent on your own valu-
ation. Besides these taxes mentioned, the town or
city authorities may levy and collect such other
taxes for town and city purposes as they, in their
wisdom, may deem necessary and these extra taxes
often amount to much more than the regular taxes
do. You are taxed for sanitary purposes, for po-
lice regulations, you are taxed in the form of license
for doing any and all kinds of business. The store-
keeper is taxed in the form of a license to sell
goods, the butcher must pay thirty-five cents for
each cow (beef) he kills. This I believe is called
the brand tax, and he must report the brand to the
marshall under penalty. The sewing machine
man, the book agent, insurance men and nearly all
mechanics must pay a tax in the form of a license
to do business. The real estate man must pay
about seventy-five dollars a year to follow his business, and costs the man who sells whiskey from
six hundred to two thousand dollars a year, besides numerous fines to engage in that nefarious
business. I have not learned if the authorities tax
Ministers of the Gospel in the way of a license or

not, but I rather guess that if any person escapes taxation or license, they do.

LAWYERS AND DOCTORS.

Legal fees are high and the less you have to do with either profession, the better for you and your purse, for while lawyers, notaries and squires' fees are high, doctors fees, in my judgement are extraordinary high, while many of them are no doubt good physicians and understand their business, one thing is very certain, they all know to perfection the art of charging, and they invariable exercise that knowledge whenever opportunity offers. The only difference is, you can, and generally do know what a lawyer is going to charge you, while you are entirely at the mercy of a doctor.

FEES

Of county officials are not extravagantly high, not much, if any higher than they are in the North but township officers and Justices of the Peace are about double what they are in the Northern States for the same service.

CONSTABLE FEES AND POWERS

Are also very much higher and greater here than they are North. Constables, or as they are here called marshalls, have the same powers in their respective towns and districts, (bailiwicks) as the sheriff has in the county, and they are all empowered to act as Deputy Sheriffs and receive the same pay and a salary besides for patrolling certain beats or districts. Summons in case of debt are seldom used, but instead thereof, a capias or warrant is used both in civil and criminal cases, and as a general thing, heroic treatment is put in force by attachment of person or property and the cases are disposed of quickly, they know nothing of stay of execution or any other kind of stay. If they can be had at all, it must be by an arrangement between the parties, either before or after judgement is obtained. There is no imprisonment for simple debt between man and man, but they do imprison for fines, public fees or anything pertaining to the county or State.

HOMESTEAD LAWS.

They do have for actual settlers or residents of the State. These laws, however are vague and complicated and the machinery of them, so cumbrous and expensive that in ninety-nine cases out of a hundred it costs less to pay the debt than to take advantage of the law. The fact is that nearly all the

LAWS

Of Florida seem to have been made by and for the lawyers. All of them seem to have two sides and both appear to be right, and unless you have the clearest kind of a case, you had better settle it before going before a Justice or getting into the court.

MORALITY OF THE PEOPLE.

Taking the commonwealth as a whole and considering that this is comparatively a new country, that it is filling up rapidly with people of all classes from different parts of the United States with a good sprinkling of foreigners, the people are moral and rather well behaved.   There are some rough and uncouth people, it is true, but you will find such in all communities, particularly so where society is in a formative state and composed of people from almost everywhere.   People here are quick to resent an insult and some of them are hot blooded and will shoot pretty quickly, but a stranger coming here and conducting himself properly and in a becoming manner, is just as safe from harm as he is, or would be in any other place in the United States, and a great deal more so than he would be in many places I know of, however there are plenty of SHARP MEN here, who will take advantage of you in the way of a trade and unless you go a little slow and investigate properly, these men will have your money, legally or otherwise, before you know much about them or Florida either for that matter.   The better plan is when you go to Florida, say but little, especially about yourself or your business, keep your eyes and ears open, learn all you can and from whom you can.   There is a great deal to be learned about the ins and outs of the country from the old negroes, both men and women, who have lived for years in the State and who, as a general thing, have no special interest in selling land or orange groves, and they are nearly all communicative, and you can draw from them much valuable information, especially about the quality of land, what has been raised on it and what can be raised and how it is done. You can then draw your own conclusions, and form your judgement accordingly. I know that these smart alex's in Florida will hoot and ridicule the idea of getting information from the negroes on agricultural subjects, but look for a moment, who has a better right or better opportunity to know than they, for the negros do nearly all the work of farming and otherwise and most of them are smart enough to know how much labor it requires to do certain things and they are observant and imitative too, and when you take them all for ignoramuses, you are very apt to get misled. It is true that the negros as a class are not smart, but there are smart ones among them.

After you have learned all you can, then do not buy too quickly, better miss a chance or two than get bit or make a mistake. Remember sociablility as a general thing, stops short as soon as you have fastened up your money, and remember also that while there are many chances to invest and make money, it is not all gold that glitters, nor is it all Florida sand lots that will pay to invest in.

Prices of articles that are daily used are about as follows :

Flour per barre', $7 00 ; flour per pound, four cents ; corn meal per pound, two and one half to three cents ; corn grits per pound, two and one-half to three cents; oat meal per

pound, three cents ; rye flour per pound, four cents ; buck
wheat per pound, ten cents ; salt per sack, G. A., $2.00 ;
salt per bushel, G. A., $1.00, white sugar per pound, ten
cents ; browe sugar per pound, nine cents ; loaf sugar per
pound, twenty cents ; coffee (best). per pound, forty cents ;
coffee (inferior), per pound, fifteen to thirty cents ; dried
peaches per pound, (best) fifteen to thirty cents ; dried ap-
p'es per pound' ten to twenty cents ; dried b'ackberries per
pound, twenty-five cents ; prunes, fifteen to twenty-five
cents ; canned fruit, dry goods and clothing about the same
as in the North ; chickens each, fort cents to $1.00 ; turkeys,
$1 50 to $3.00 ; venison per pound, fifteen aul twent; five
cents ; quai's per dozen, $1.50 and $2 00 ; fresh fish per
pound, five to fifteen cents ; eggs per dozen, twenty-five to
fifty cents ; Irish potatoes by the bushel, $2.00 to $4.00 ;
sweet po'atoes per bushel, fifty cents to $1 00 ; tomatoes per
peck, seventy five cen's to $1 00 ; snap beans per peck,
seventy five cents to $1.00 ; cow peas per peck, fifty to
seventy-five cents ; onions per peck, eigh'y cents to $1.20 ;
oranges each, two to five cents ; grape fru't each, five to ten
cents ; lemons per dozen, forty cents ; b manas per bunch.
seventy five cents to $3 00 ; strawberries a box. (about a
pint), twenty-five cents to $1.50 ; huckleberries per box, ten
to twenty-five cents ; peaches per crate, (about a half bushe')
$ 50 to $5.00 ; hay per one hundred pounds, $1 25 to $2.00
apples per barrel, (Northern). $4 00 to $6 00 ; corn per
sack, two bushels, $1.40 t) $1 80 ; oats per sack, [four
bushels) $2 10 to $2 60); wheat per bushel, (chicken feed)
three to four cents ; wheat ser-nings, (chicken feed), two to
three cents ; lumber, rough and dimension per 1,000 fee'.
$12.00 to $14 00 ; flooring, plained and matched per thousand
feet, $17 00 to $18 00 ; shingles per thousand feet, (cypress)
$4.50 to $6 00 ; shingle, (yellow pine) per thousand feet,
$3 00 to $5 00 ; wood. per stran, $1 50 to $2.00 ; wood per
cord, $3.00 th $5.00 ; beef per pound, native 5 to 15 cents;
Northern beef per pound, 15 to 25 cents; pork, 12 to 15
cents; mutton, 15 to 20 cents; veal, 15 to 20 cents. About
the same average prices are paid for all you buy in Florida.

LANDS.

Nine-tenths of all the up lands in Florida arworthless for agricultural or horticultural purposes, that is they are so sandy that nothing will grow on the land in its natural state, it however, answers as a good base for manure and fertilizers, and when properly brought up by these agents, will produce vegetables, fruits, and such other things as are described in this book.

The value of these lands is determined much more by location than quality. Wild lands (unimproved lands) several miles away from towns and railroads are comparatively low in price, while the same quality or kind of land near towns or close to railroads are held at enormous prices You can now begin to see where big money is made. Get ahead of the railroads, buy your land cheap, or at nominal figures, lay out your town, boom it up any way you can, induce some persons to buy lots and build, start a store no matter what kind of a store— five or ten pounds each of coffee, sugar, tobacco, bacon, and a little grits and flour will make a good outfit, you do not care if you sell these goods at a profit or not, that is not your point to be made. Your point is to get settlers, as soon as you have a few inhabitants you will give some railroad company a good slice of your land just to get them to run their road through your lands. These railroad companies are quick to see where money is to be made ; the offer of land in sufficient quantities will bring a railroad or branch almost anywhere in Florida. Railroads are easily built here. If the

company sees any money in it straightway, the
road is built, then the balance of your land will
bring more than a hundred times more than you
paid for it. You have made big money and are
the big man of the town; the railroad company
has made money, not only by running their road
into or through your town, but have been paid the
cost of making their road many times over by the
sale of the land you gave them for running your
way, now neither you or the railroad oompany
(especially) cares much who sticks. You do not
care much for the end man.

When the Northern man gets on to Florida soil,
his first impressions are after looking about him;
well this is Florida as it is; the "Land of Sunshine
and Flowers. The sunshine you have, that is
here. The flowers I do not see, but I do see sand
pure (poor) white sand. "Is all your land so
sandy?" Oh, no! (first fib). We have plenty of
the richest black loam (2) you ever saw, and we
raise the biggest kind of vegetable" (3). Your impressions begin to change very soon from this kind
of talk, but without the talk the impressions run
in about this way: What in the world can people
in this sandy country do for a living, certainly
nothing will grow on this land without first putting
on manure or fertilizer, about as much as you can
in any case get off it, and where is the stuff to
make fertilizer of? Very little grass can grow
here, there is no limestone, there is no natural fer-

tilizer, these pine leaves are no good, the fact is there is no soil at all, this sand seems to run clear to the bottom, and if left to yourself, in ninety cases out of one hundred you would turn away and leave the State in disgust, go home and report that Florida was nothing but a sandy desert or a wilderness of pine barrens, lakes, ponds and swamps, and was not fit for any person to live in, that it always was the habitations of Indians and wild beasts and all manner of pests and your opinton would be, that it should forever remain so, and I am not sure but what your idea of the land and country is about, at least three-quarters correct.

HEAT.

Heat in summer, especially before the summer rains set in, is almost unbearable. The thermometer for weeks is high up in the nineties, frequently above one hundred degrees, (farenheit) during nearly the entire day, falling at night to about eighty-five degrees. The only thing that makes this climate endurable at all in summer, is the nearly constant breeze or mild wind which seems to cool the air a little. As to hot days and cool nights in Florida in summer, it looks well on paper especially the cool nights, and when you read about them, in imagination you feel kind of comfortable, perhaps in the enjoyment of them in the future. Let me say right here that if there was or is any truth in the saying that distance lends enchantment to the view, it certainly applies with full force in this case.

This cool night business answers first-class for advertising, but when you come to test it, you will here again find that there is always some truth in these advertising circulars, but while there are some cool nights, you will find some very warm ones and a big majority of them are uncomfortably hot, so much so that it is impossible to sleep on account of the heat. If you attempt to sleep in a room or place where the air or breeze does not pass over you; should you go to sleep at all, which is doubtful, you will very soon wake up with perspiration oozing out at every pore; the nights are hot, no use trying to disguise the fact, how can they be otherwise; the thermometer up to ninety-eight or one hundred during nearly the entire day and not below eighty or eighty-five during the whole twenty-four hours with the ground or sand so hot that in five minutes your feet would be blistered were you to walk on it in your bare feet; let me ask in the name of common sense, how can the nights be anything but hot. Now then, if you still have doubts about this thing, just you come to Orange county. I name this particular county because it is claimed to be the banner county of the State and I am not sure but what it is, in fact I know it is if booming can make it so. Well you just come to Orlando, Kissimmee, Eustis or Tavares about the middle of June and try it, be sure and get a room where the wind does not blow on you. You better be sure and have a mosquito bar over you, and a good one too, or you will hardly know where to place the blame of your not sleeping. You might possibly think that fighting the mosquitos had made you uncomfortably warm. After you have made this experiment, I rather think you will agree with me that they do have hot nights in Florida, sure enough! And you will probably exclaim as one of old, "surely the half has not been told!" I might add right here that Orange county and particularly the places named above. have fewer mosquitos and other pests than any other part of the State. This may be so, (I do not believe it), but if these are the good places, I do not think you will ever care to visit the other places; you will be thoroughly satisfied in a short time that they do have hot days and nights, mosquitos and pests in abundance in Orange county. Florida, and if there is the garden spot (there are other places just the same in every respect) and comparatively clear of pests, what must the rest of the State be.

TOWNS AND CITIES.

Jacksonville, Duval county, is the metropolis or grand ENTRE POT of the State. It is to Florida about what Philadelphia is to Pennsylvania. As nearly as I can ascertain it has a population of about twenty-five thousand inhabitants. In the winter season the population is much larger. All the railroads of the South centre here; no matter where you wish to go in Florida, you will probably start from Jacksonville. It also has water communications by the way of the mouth of St. John River, connecting wlth the Atlantic Ocean. distance about thirteen miles; also water communication with the interior of the State by the St. Johns and Ocklawaha rivers. Steamers, ships and water craft of all shapes and sizes line her wharves trom all countries and nations. To say the least of Jacksonville, she is a busy, bustling little city with street cars, electric lights, manufacturies, and all kinds of business in full blast. A great many of her business men are from the North, with a good sprinkling of foreigners, Jews and a few natives. Goods aud merchandise of almost every description can be bought in Jacksonville almost as cheaply as in the Northern cities, provided you happen to strike the right parties, but there are plenty of sharpers there as there are in all other large places and it is well enough for strangers to be on their guard while in Jacksonville, especially after night. Many a man has been heard of last in that city, although it is no worse in that respect or do I think it is as bad as some other cities much farther up North.

TALLAHASSEE

Is the captal ot the State. If the public building and the public business were removed from Tallahassee, there would not be very much left.

GAINESVILLE

Is quite a neat little city and has a good deal of push and vim. It is the county seat of Alachua county and is said to contain about eight thousand inhabitants. This town has some as fine buildings as there are in the State, many of which are built of brick.

OCALA

Is the county seat of Marion county. It is rather an old town not more than half as large as Gainesville, which is perhaps the wealthiest town in the State of her size or according to her population. Pensacola, Apalachicola, Cedar Keys, Key West, Tampa, Bartow and many others are towns of some note here and are much more notorious in the North than they are when you are in them.

ORLANDO

Is the county seat of Orange county; now claims our attention. This town or city, if we can believe the citizens thereof, especially the real estate men, is almost an Eden, but taking the facts as they are Orange county is about eighty miles long North and South, and about fifty miles wide, East and West; it's shape is amorphus, being very irregular; I cannot give figures that are reliable about its population, therefore will not venture a guess. There are several good sized and growing towns in the county. Eustis, Tavares, Sanford, Maitland. Winter Park, Apopka City, Wildwood, Zellwood,

Ocoee, Gotha, Longwood, Pine Castle, and last but not least by any means, is Kissimmee City, located on the boarders of Tohopekaliga Lake and claims a population of twelve hundred inhabitants, but now again to Orlando. It, a very few years ago, was but a sorry little village. notwithstanding it was a county seat, six or seven years ago a few smart enterprising men seeing the situation bought up quite a body of land in the village and vicinity and began to boom (advertise) the town; their venture proved a success financially and otherwise and now Orlando is second to none in the State for its growth, and the amount of business it does, for its size, and bids fair in a few years to outstrip all other towns in the State, Jacksonville alone excepted. Many new and apparently thriving towns have sprung up within the last three or four years and where the wild beasts and Indians used to roam now the shriek and whistle of the locomotive is heard; you naturally ask what has made all this change? The answer is, speculation and specution only, advertising and booming by speculators.

BOOMING.

Booming as I understand it, and as it is, is to talk up the place, write and advertise it all over the country, tell all the good you know about it, be very particular to write or say nothing bad about it, but tell what has been and can be done; in telling about what can be done, here you can draw on your imagination to almost any extent and not be blamed for lying, perhaps I should have said prevarication, as that term is not quite so harsh but I think the first word is the better one in this case, and when they tell you of how much some person has made since they came to Florida, they always get the figures as big as possible; the people living outside of the State do not know if you are telling or advertising the truth or not; say nothing about the mosquitos, sand, flies, fleas, red bugs, bad water or anything about any of the pests that abound all over the State. Should the boomers be asked or written to about these things, the answer must, and will be evasive or something like the people of Ohio said about the milk sickness, it was always over in the next county; you could never get to the place where it would actually be acknowledged. They are in the State, but principally along the coast or down in the big cypress swamps where no person lives anyhow, or any other place than the particular place you are writing or talking about but they must be mighty scarce about it, and if it should so happen that some man should chance to raise some new seedling fruit or berry, be it a peach, orange or a strawberry that has been pushed and nurtured into producing a fair fruit, then take hold of that, have it published in all the papers far and near, have circulars printed and sown broadcast all over the land, make this particular thing, fruit or whatever it may be, fully as large as it really is, and if they succeed in fully describing it, draw a little on the imagination and be sure to figure it out so as to show how immensely profitable it will be, that is, it will sell for so much per quart or bushel, as the case may be, but never say a word about the care it must have or the costs of raising the fruits or berries, and as you are doing this all principally through newspapers and circulars, there is not much danger of people asking questions about the cost of production, taking for granted that it is a natural thing for such a fruit or berry to grow that way in Florida, show also by circulars and otherwise that the price of lands, lots, etc., double in value about every three months, in no case make it over a year; this is booming sure enough!

There are many towns in the State, most of which are thriving, just in the proportion to the way they are boomed. A description of one boom is sufficient for all, so you see that booming and speculation go hand in hand.

Nearly all the new towns in the State are started as above described and very many of the older towns are given a fresh start by the same process. When adjoining lands can be had in large quantities, take for example St. Augustine, (Augusteen) this town is said to be, and I believe is the oldest town in the United States, but until very recently was not much more than a mere barracks on the sandy coast, but a few years ago speculators with capital took hold of the old town, bought adjoining lands and went to booming the town and now the place is quite a city, and the surrounding lands that even four or five years ago were comparatively worthless, sell for hundreds, and in some cases for thousands of dollars per acre, not because it is valuable for producing anything, for it is as poor as poverty itself, but simply because it is near St. Augustine.

Hundreds of persons are thus making money in Florida, and the more money you have to start with the more you can make, provided your speculations turn out favorably to you. Here again I will say, that with very few exceptions the man who has but little or no ready cash, can do much better almost any other place than in Florida.

Now because I have not mentioned or named other towns, the reader must not think that there are no other towns in the State for there are hundreds of them and some not mentioned are larger and perhaps much better than some that are named To write them up separately with their history and growth, with their advantages, (if they have any) and their disadvantages, would make a volume or book of such a size that it would be too cumbrous to handle, besides such a work would be very tedious and entirely too prosy to read, for when you know the history and booming of one town, city or place, it will fit to all of them with very little variation—very few exceptions to this as a rule. Towns and cities seem to take root and grow here

about as well, if not better than anything else I
know of, particularly for the first few years of their
existence, especially if they are well fertilized with
proper booming.   This is about the only fertilizer
that I know of that will cause towns and cities to
grow, and if it is properly applied, it and it alone
will pay the purchaser thereof.   Here again however, look out and do not be the end man or you
will get left.

NEWSPAPERS.

Newspapers are numerous here, the fact is it is
almost impossible to boom a town or place without
the printing press, and as it is much cheaper to buy
a printing press and hire a printer than to pay for
the necessary amount of printing needed in the
enterprise; about the first thing in a new town is a
so-called newspaper generally owned by the company and apparently managed by one man; the
profits from the paper at first is nothing, the expenses however, are not very heavy; as soon as
people begin to come to the place and invest, start
up little stores and embark in such business as
must necessarily follow the people; advertising is
resorted to, and when you put an advertisement in a
paper in Florida, you will find the price something
like the doctor's bills, however it must go in, thus
the paper soon pays the expenses of running it and
thus the company gets their advertising for comparatively nothing, and can print what they please
and can draw it mild or strong to suit the occasion.

The subscription price of newspapers here are not any more than in the North.

You will notice that a great many things that appear in the papers as local matter on close inspection look like advertisements, for example nearly all the newspapers note the transfers of lands taking place weekly; some of these are noted as taking place on certain days, when the facts are the transfer had been made several months before and been so noted at the time. These things are of more frequent occurrence in the summer season, which is the dull time, but something must be done to make the people abroad believe that the business is booming in Florida the whole year around. This has its effect in inducing people to come here and who ever comes, it makes business for some person—the liveryman, the hotel and boarding house keeper, real estate men and the railroads. This again makes items for the newspapers and thus it goes on adinfinitum; again when a certain fruit or vegetable has been grown of rather an unusual size, flavor or quality, advertisements in the form of local matter appears in all the papers far and near and many times repeated in even the same paper; the attention of the whole State and the United States, so far as they can be reached, is called to this particular thing when the article in itself nearly always proves to be but very common in the end.

Just now the Bidwell peach is the fruit that is

going to revolutionize the fruit business in Florida.
It is said they ripen about the first of June—some
two weeks earlier than any other, and are said to
be of superior flavor and quality; a few of this
variety were sent to New York market this season
for the first time, and were sold at the rate of 27
dollars per bushel, (a good price for peaches) sure
enough! It is not said how many peaches were
sent to the New York market, or is it necessary,
but the probabilities are that there were but few,
the language least implies that, when closely scan-
ned, we notice they were sold at the rate of twenty-
seven dollars per bushel. Now even this, although
they are making such a blow about it, is not much
better than raising strawberries, and selling them
at home here for a dollar and a quarter a box, or
sending them to the Eastern markets at the rate of
forty or fifty dollars a bushel. These things have
been done time and again. The only wonder to
to me is that the peaches did not bring a larger
price in New York, for there are a good many
people interested in the sale of Florida lands and
town lots who live in that big city, and yet I have
the first man or woman to see who got rich or made
money in this State by raising and selling strawberries and peaches. Another good quality of this
Bidwell peach is that it bears fruit the third year
from planting. I have not been able to learn if
this means from the pit or bud. About the whole
thing is, some person has a big lot of peach trees

for sale; this kind only grows on Florida soil, and some person else has a big lot of that kind of soil for sale they; thus, as it were, splice teams and boom this particular peach for a particular purpose, knowing that there are a great many people in the North who have money to invest and this looks as if there was big money it, they go to Florida, invest in land, buy the trees, plant their orchard, and await results. The tree raiser and the land man have made their points and unless you sell your peach orchard while the boom is up, you will likely be the end man, and in any case some person will be the end man; so this business goes on, if not one thing it is another. It may be beans, tomatoes, peaches, cocoanuts, pine apples, oranges, bananas, cucumbers, melons or indeed almost anything to entice people to part with their money.

N. B.—I have just learned from a reliable nurseryman, that the Bidwell peach is a seedling cross of the Peento and honey peach, and is a better peach than either of the other two, and it ought, to be worth anything.

HEALTH.

From general reports and published accounts in Newspapers, particularly by those interested in Florida, the State is a paradise and a sure restorer of health to invalids of we may say the entire outside of the world, and all who are sick or have any kind of ailment, all they have to do, is to get into the general climate of Florida ; it is a panacea for all the ills that human flesh is heir to, and when you get under its influence straightway, you become hale and hearty, and will add to your days many years. The facts in the case, however do uot warrant the assertions. A large proportion of the natives (white) are lean and do not look healthy and the women particularly are, to say the least of it, delicate and a large percentage of the people who have came to Florida, have some ailment and are here for their health. The result is you see but comparatively few stout and healthy looking people ; about all the healthy looking people you do see here are those who came from other States with plenty of money in their pockets, either to see sights, speculate or both, and very few of these remain the entire season. They come in the fall of the year and return in the spring, thus enjoying the pleasant winter here, and the summers at some cool watering place or summer resort in the North. Now with regard to the sanitary condition of things here, according to my judgement and observation about the only persons who receive benefit in health by coming to Florida, are those who are afflicted with pulmonary or asthmatic diseases persons having incipient or consumption in the first stages, and before the disease has taken a firm hold, may be benefited by spending a winter here, and thus avoid the extreme cold winter of the North, but for any other kind of disease, almost any other place is about as good as Florida. Nine-tenths of the people who come here for their health, for all the benefit they receive might just as well remain at home and thus save their time and money.

DISEASES IN FLORIDA.

There are no special or prevalent fatal diseases here, there is, however, a kind of low type of fever that prevails to a considerable extent all over the State, that in almost any other place or State would be named or called malarial fever, (but they have no malaria in Florida) People here take cold just about as readily and as easily as in most other places, and they sometimes get pretty sick and have to send for a doctor. This in almost any other place or State would, be called pneumonia, (but they do not have any pneumonia here either.) Many of the inhabitants here frequently get what they call hot and cold spells and sometimes they shake a little too,—for these spells they use quinine. This disease anywhere else would be called chills and fevers, but they do not have any ague in Florida ; nobody ever heard of a case in the whole State, and while the weather is very hot, nearly every person will tell you there never has been a sun stroke known to occur in the State, nothwith-standing there has been numerous deaths from what is called nervous prostration, the symptons of which are identical with those of sun stroke. There are frequent cases of small pox and sometimes it assumes the form of an epidemic, and is just as fatal as elsewhere. Measels, whooping cough and all the diseases that children and even grown people are subject to, are here, and I cannot see that there is much, if any difference in this respect from other States and places. Yellow fever has been in the State a number of times, and so has cholera. It is barely possible that many of the diseases here do not assume so malignant a form as they do in some other places, but after all is said about the diseases here that can be said, people do die here and of about the same diseases that they die of in other places, but to say that Florida has about the same diseases that other parts of the country has, detracts very much from her reputation as a health resort. The facts are that Florida is a good winter resort and when that is said it is nearly all that can be truthfully said about the State.

You will find out, it you do not already know it, that everything here is magnified several or more times. The transient visitor generally has these magnifying glasses fixed on his eyes before coming here and hardly ever stays long enough in the State to get them off. He therefore sees only one side of the picture and that always the bright side particularly if he has plenty of money, but let him settle down among the people and become one of them (as it were,) the glass and glamour soon wears off and the realities begin to appear, and the longer he remains the more he finds out, and when the magnifying glasses are entirely removed, then, and not until then can he see "Florida as it is." The wonder to me is that a book similar to this one has not been written long since. The only reason I can give is about like this: That parties become interested in speculation and as many of them have been to a certain extent taken in (so to speak) and on the principal that misery loves company and perhaps with a view that something will turn up by which they can better their condition in the end. This is the only reason that seems to be plausible that "Florida as it is" or something that would give the people of the whole country the true light on this subject has not been written.

SAND OR FLORIDA ITCH.

This is something seldomly heard of outside of the State and the people or inhabitants say very little about it. You know itch is a kind of disease or disorder that is not very popular anyhow, and persons who are afflicted with it, will not say much about it. This disease is not at all fatal or does it seem to be contagious, but it is very disagreeable to have. What produces this itch I do not know; it may be the sand (and I think it is), which is as fine as emery that gets into the pores of the skin, or it may be the climate, heat and sand combined produces it, one thing is certain, very few people escape it, especially those who remain during the summer. You hear nothing of it in the winter season.

There is also something in either the soil (sand) or climate that causes any little scratch or hurt that you may get, and very often without, to become sore and very much inflamed, and unless proper remedies are applied at once, cause a good deal of pain and suffering. What this is I have not been able to find out from any person; if the doctors know they will not tell, and now when you come to put these things all together and begin to analyze, it does seem rather strange that, from some cause or causes, will and does cause eruptions and breaking out and causes sores and boils all over the surface of the body. That these causes should or would cure and make healthy the internal organs when diseased, this is a question that I will leave for the reader to figure out. This, however inconsistent it may appear, is claimed for this Florida climate or something else. This is not a whit more inconsistent than scores of other things that are claimed for this "Land of Sunshine and Flowers," but as before stated, Florida has a climate peculiarly her own, hence these seeming inconsistencies; you will understand these things much better after a residence of a year or two in the aforesaid climate, and particularly so, should you have the Florida itch and attempt to sleep with the thermometer at ninety, at 9 o'clock at night and no breeze blowing and surrounded by a cloud of mosquitos, each one presenting his bill and singing at your ears, "blood, blood."

RAILROADS.

The principal of which is the Florida Railway and Navigation Company. Their system of roads extend nearly all over the State; their track is standard guage. I believe all the other roads in the State are narrow guage except the T. O. & A., which is an extension of the F. R. & N., but owned by a different company. The Jacksonville, Tampa and Key West, and South Florida Railway companies have their roads completed and cars running nearly the entire length of the State North and South. The tracks on these roads are all narrow guage. The Florida Southern also has a road in running order from Jacksonville to Cedar Keys. There are quite a number of short roads and many now building, most of which are narrow guage; I presume however, that inside of a year or two at least, all the principal railroads in the State will be changed to standard guage. It is an easy matter to build a railroad in Florida; no rock to blow and remove, no big cuts or big fills, no tunnels to bore and very few bridges to build— all that is to be done is to get two or three dozen or more Italians (always to be had) and have them shovel up a road of sand, level off the top, put down the ties, put on the rails and rolling stock, and then charge five cents a mile for passengers and from two to five cents per hundred pounds per mile for freight. This does not look like speculation, does it? It does look a good deal like extortion though, don't it? Where two railroads come into competition, rates are more reasonable, but still much higher than in the North.

WHAT WE EAT, AND WHERE WE GET IT.

The inhabitants of Florida are a good deal like other people concerning their diet. They are just as fond of good eatables as any person else, but the best things cannot always be had, they therefore eat what ever they have and get it wherever they can. They generally have plenty of Florida beef, and some Florida pork ; they usually have plenty of sweet potatoes (not always) and some Irish potatoes (in season) ; they have snap beans, cow peas, cucumbers, tomatoes, water and mush melons, turnips, some cabbage, and a few other vegetables, they also have oranges and guavas plenty when they dont freeze ; a few lemons, bananas, pine apples, some strawberries, and few other fruits and berries in certain localities. These things are produced at home.

Wheat, flour, corn meal, corn grits, ham, bacon, apples, and nearly all the substantials of life they eat, but all these things must come from abroad. They also eat dried fruits, jams, jellies, canned fruits and meats. These are all imported. Good butter cannot be had here ; the natives butter is little, if any better than grease, and by the time Northern butter gets down here, it is not much better. The native beef during the greater part of the year is very poor, and to ship Northern beef here either on the hoof or in quarters, is kind of sorry meat too.

Now as to Florida beef. To have it, all that is to be done is to kill a cow, no matter in what condition, whether fat or poor, when cut up it is Florida beef. I have seen plenty of cows (cattle) killed here and ate that in the North would have been called very poor stock cattle. The cattle that are killed for beef are not all of this class, but in the winter and spring very many are quite poor; in the summer and fall they are in better condition, and I have seen them so fat that there was some signs of tallow on the kidneys. The native pork is much better than the beef, and yet I have seen hogs killed here for pork that there was not enough of lard in them to fry them; these however are the exceptions. There are some fine fat little hogs here and they make rather nice eating. (if you don't like the fat little hog you may read it, the little fat hog.

As to the vegetables grown here, very few of them are first-class. They nearly all have a toughness about them, the cabbage particularly so. The tomatoes, cucumbers, turnips, radishes, &c., have none of that crispness about them that first-class vegetables have; even the watermelons have a soggy appearance and taste. Oranges are good, first-class than which I suppose none better in the known world. Bananas, what few are raised here are a fair quality; so are the pine apples. Sweet potatoes are only fair, more like yams in the

North. Irish potatoes, as a general crop, are not
a success either in quantity or quality. Nearly all
the lard and butter used in the State, is shipped
here from the North, and you can form some kind
of an idea of the condition it is in when it reaches
our market and remains sometimes for weeks in a
temperature with the thermometer up in the nineties
As to light bread, you seldom see it ; a kind of bread
called light, (that is it is light in weight) is made
and sold by the bakers—hot bread in the shape
of biscuits three times a day or as often as you eat,
Florida beef, corn grits, condensed milk and butter-
ine with either sweet or Irish potatoes and coffee or
tea is the usual meal ; sometimes the meat is omit-
ted at breakfast when fish (mullet) takes the place
thereof. Sometimes this bill of fare is varied for
supper or dinner for that matter, and you will make
a right good meal on bologna sausage, cold biscuits or crackers, using for drink pure c—; I almost wrote cold lake water, and sometimes you will
get something that is real palatable in the shape of
a boned catfish, stuffed opossum or roast of venison
the fact of this whole business is, the native Flori-
dian and for that matter all who are in the State,
eat whatever they have that is eatable and gets it
wherever they can. They get it honestly if possible
to do so, but they all get a living somehow. As a
general thing all the butters, jellies, jams and
dainties are missing here ; there is one production
that there is a good deal of noise about here.

THE CASAVA PLANT,

A root from which tapioca is made. I think perhaps this is like many other things here, for I have made diligent search and inquiry to find out where and how it grows, and have thus far entirely failed to see any of it, or any person that has seen it, yet it may be growing somewhere in the State and some day may be profitable, who knows !

FERTILITY OF THE SOIL.

Speaking generally, the soil of Florida is of a poor kind of quality. There is not one acre in twenty, and I doubt if there is one in a hundred that will pay to cultivate in anything at all without fertilizer, except the reclaimed marsh lands. Everything you plant, (sweet potatoes excepted) must be fertilized, and it does not hurt the sweet potatoes to fertilize them a little if you would get a good crop, and unless you do fertilize you will get no crop, and with all the care, cultivation and cost, the best thing you can do your crop when raised will sell for very little, if any more than it cost to raise it, in any case it will not anymore than pay for your labor and attention, besides the cost of raising as before stated. There is nothing made here in either agricultural or horticultural pursuits, and nearly all of that kind of work that is done in the State is done in small patches and lots, if nursed, fed and fertilized all it will bear or take up, then it may be only a patch fifteen or twenty feet square that has received the very best attention and has produced a big crop for the size of the place, now an estimate is made on what can be grown on an acre, but nothing is said about the care, attention, &c., thus leaving people at a distance under the impression that by ordinary cultivation such crops can be raised almost anywhere in the State, when the facts are that by ordinary cultivation nothing at all can be raised; why the land is so poor in many places that even weeds will not grow.

FERTILIZER.

Nearly everything here is utilized for fertilizer, and any and everything in the shape of manures and droppings of man, beast and fowls are utilized. A very good way to fertilize a small plot of ground, is to fence it, then have some person that has a small heard of cattle or a bunch of hogs, pen them in this lot, (this is called cowpenning land.) If you can keep the stock on long enough they will fertilize it so that vegetables and even a little corn will grow on it. Men or parties who have a large bunch of cattle proceed in this way to prepare their lands for orange groves, and has proved to be a success in more cases than one. If you have to hire your cowpenning, it will cost you about one dollar per month per head, then the cattle are penned every night.

Another way is to gather all the cow chips (droppings) or buy them; they sell for about fifty cents a barrel; pulverize or have them pulverized, and apply on the surface of the ground. Horse manure is much used for early vegetables; bones are gathered up, broken, ground or burned, and then applied as a top dressing; the contents of outhouses, sinks, slops, refused meats, fish offalls, anything that has, or seems to have any fertilizing properties in them, are all thrown on the compost heap or pile and afterwards used as fertilizer. After consuming all the domestic fertilizer that can be had, then if the parties have any money they buy commercial fertilizer Many haul muck from the swamps or muckbeds when not too far off, this, however is of doubtful utility, while it doubtless improves the quality of the soil, it generally costs more than it comes to. Fertilizing is the key note to the raising of all the fruits and vegetables of Florida, and without it nothing of any account can be raised. It must be applied several times a year and that abundantly and without stint. All the yarns and stories to the contrary notwithstanding.

CHURCHES.

There are church organizations in nearly all the towns and many of them have several church organizations. The colored people also have churches in nearly, if not all the places that the whites have. The negros and whites never worship together in the same church. The Methodists seem to predominate; the Presbtyerians and Baptists seem to be about alike in numercial strength; there are some Episcopalians and a good many Catholics. The negroes are divided between the Methodist and Baptists. It rather seems to be fashionable to belong to a church, and in a great many instances that I know of church members prostitute the church or use their membership for quite another purpose than it was intended- . A few of the worst scalawags that the writer knows of are church members who partook of the Holy Sacrament of the Lord's Supper on Sunday morning, took parties in the afternoon of the same day to show and try to sell them land, and who, on the following week did arrange a villainous scheme to beat a party out of a large sum of money and he succeeded in the scheme to a very considerable extent. Another case, that of a local preacher on a certain Sabbath morning took a party to see a lot arranged, then went straight to church and into the pulpit and preached a sermon. Many other such tricks of a similar character are of almost daily occurrence, and it is not much thought of, only accounted rather smart. These things are always done in such a way that there is not much chance for the party that gets beaten, the laws are such that a man can do almost anything he has a mind to in Florida; if he has a little money he need have no particular fear of getting into trouble, or if he does get into trouble, his money will get him out.

One day in riding in the cars on the South Florida Railroad. in conversation with a gentleman

who had lived in the State for a considerable length
of time, and who was then living there and for
all I know is living in the State yet; in the course
of our conversation he remarked that there was
more solid lying done in Florida to the square foot
of land than in any other country or State that he
knows of. I did not know then whether to believe
him or not, but since living here for some time and
doing business with the people, I am satisfied that
he spoke the truth, and might have made it strong-
er yet, and still been within bounds, and yet the
lying is done in such a way that at the time you
cannot tell or detect it. It is done by magnifying
everything and drawing on the imagination to
complete the picture, and by taking small plots
and magnifying them into acres, as for example
a certain man raised so many quart of strawberries
on a square rod of ground, it having the best of
cultivation, attention and fertilization, such as
could not have been given to even an acre of
ground, much less five or ten acres; the yield on
the small plot was immense of course, it being all
got up for an advertisement. Well, this small plot
will be magnified in a very short space of time to
perhaps twenty acres, and the yield perhaps increased a little, and possibly directly you will be
told that the man raised this crop the first year,
after clearing wild land and that he gave it no
special attention either. You do not know and
have no means of knowing whether it is true or

not, and just as likely as not the very fellow who
has told you all this stuff is an actual active
church member, or in other words a wolf in sheep's
clothing. I don't wish the reader to understand
that I am finding fault with the church for I revere
and love it; I am only trying to show you a certain class of men who are using the church to ac-
complish their nefarious ends, and do not understand me to say or mean that all the man or members of churches in Florida are of this class, very
far from it, you will find just as honorable and
square men here to deal with as you will find anywhere, both in and out of church, but being fore-
warned ought to be forearmed; do not invest too
quickly and do not bestow your confidence without
some previous knowledge.

Another way of exaggerating is about like this,
a man has a piece or tract of land for sale, he may
want to sell ever so badly, he will probably tell
you here is a tract of land for which he has refused
so much money; now this may be so. In this way
he and some person else may have or has an understanding that he shall help to sell the land and
get so much when the sale is completed. In your
travels you will probably almost certainly run
across or meet the man who made the offer for the
land. It having been previously arranged, but he
he has now bought, but if he had not he would
still give that amount for it, this all looks right
and square, and if you do not watch mighty closely

and sharply, you will be caught right there by this process of lying.

There are various ways of telling things so that they resemble the truth, and having some truth mixed into the story, and the speaker being a church member or a member of some order that you know something about and seeming to be all straight who will brother you, and nearly every person he meets, that a great wonder will be, if you are not deceived, A man may be a real estate man in Florida and be a christian. but let me say right here, it takes a good deal of grace and close watching to go straight in that business and there is generally more or less room to suspect a man's christianity. When you find him engaged in the land business in a new country at least it will do no harm to watch him. Notwithstanding all that has been said and written, there are men in the land business in Florida, some of whom belong to the church and other societies, and others who do not, who will tell you about as nearly the truth as they know or understand it, and whose judgement can be taken everytime and money made by it, then there are others and plenty of them that you cannot believe one word they say, and who will fleece you every time they get a chance, some of which I could name, but I reckon I will let you do as I did, find out for yourself. Land agents in all newly developing countries are a necessity, but land sharks are of no use to any person but an injury to the business and the community in which they operate.

PROFANITY.

A large majority of the men, both white and black use cuss words, when and where they seem to be unnecessary and out of place, at least in a community that claims to be moral. Some of the native women and some that are not natives, can swear right smart too, notwithstanding all this, there are Sunday Schools in nearly all the churches with a full corps of officers. You also find a band of hope in nearly all places where there is a church and generally a Woman's Christian Temperance Union. These are all located in the towns and cities. You know, or at least I do, that the rural districts, are now, to a certain extent uninhabited, and I guess always will be. Wherever you see a half dozen houses and sometimes not more than one or two, the place is called a town, city, park, sola or something that means a great deal more than it is.

PROHIBITION.

There is quite a strong prohibition element in Florida among both whites and blacks. The law on the license business is such that the party applying for license to sell strong drinks and make people drunk, must have as signers to his petition majority of all the legal voters in the district where he proposes to sell, and any and every town, city, district or county has the right to vote once a year, whether license shall be granted in said place or not. Should license be granted in any case the said license will cost the parties in no case, less than five hundred dollars and may cost that many thousand. As I understand it, these licenses consist of three parts. First, the State license; second the district or county license, then the city or town license, the State and county license combined is three hundred dollars in all cases. The city or town license may be only two hundred dollars, no less by the statute, but the city or town authorities may by law, make the license as much higher as they choose and in a number of cases they make it so high that it almost amounts to total prohibition. The fine for selling strong drinks contrary to law is heavy, and the law is enforced about as well as any other law in the State and my observation is that all laws, particularly such as have a fine connected with them, are rigidly enforced, and in many cases summarily, I account for this in this way : That all the laws, or nearly so, that have a fine in money attached, the informant gets half the fine ; this being the case, it is a source of money making, and as there are a good many people in Florida who are too lazy to work, they watch the misdoings of others and make it profitable.

KITCHEN HELP, WASHING, &C.

Florida is a hard place for women to live in, unless their circumstances are such that they are

not obliged to work, The labor of cooking, washing and doing general house work, is much more
laborious and fatigueing than in the North. The
extreme natural heat in connection with fires necessary to do much of the household work, makes the
labor almost unendurable and the very great difficulty of getting efficient help in the house, and
enormous prices you must pay for it, puts it beyond
the reach of people in ordinary, or even moderate
circumstances, and should you be able to obtain
help at all, they (the help) must superintend or
boss the kitchen and on the least provocation, and
sometimes without any at all, they will leave you.
Ordinary kitchen work, such as cooking, washing
dishes, etc., will cost from four to ten dollars per
week, then you must furnish a separate room and
board the party, and with all the watching you
can do, they will take away (steal) fully half as
much as their wages amount to, and about half the
time, they are absent, running the street. You
must remember that the house help will in no case
do the washing and ironing; this has to be done
outside and will cost you one dollar per dozen
pieces of wearing clothes, towels, etc ; for washing
bed clothes they charge more. It must also be re-
membered that the negroes have a kind of secret
society regularly organized, including both the
men and women, and they meet regularly and fix
their own prices for doing housework, cooking,
washing, etc., and they stick right there and to the

prices fixed, so you must either do your own work, not have it done at all or pay the prices, and should you have help and turn them off for any cause, you will not be able to get any other until you agree to take back the one that you turned off. Occasionally you can get white help, but very seldomly, and when it can be had the character of the parties is generally such that you do not care to have them about you, so here again you find that unless you have plenty of money, your women folks must bear all the burden, which certainly has no tendency to improve either their health or temper as the writer very well knows. Should you hire negroes to clean house or do any other ordinary work by the day, they board themselves, come when they get ready and quit when they please, and unless you have the price fixed beforehand, they will charge you three times what they should, and if you do not pay them on the spot, they will sue you and make you pay more cost than their wages amounted to. Remember this is no fancy sketch, but the actual facts as they occur daily, so you see you must not only take the climate of Florida as you find it, but also the house help as you can get it or have no houses; true you can board, and not be bothered with house help and your washing in any case will not cost so much, but you will find that a boarding house life in Florida soon becomes monotonous. This, however is "Florida as it is," and what are you going to do about it.

There is this can be done, either conform to the habits and customs or get out of the State in the shortest space of time. Another thing can be said about the washing of clcthes, it takes twice as much washing as it does in other places, particularly in the dry season, tne nature of the soil (sand) is such that it soils clothes quickly, and garments that can be worn a whole week in the North, must here be changed two or three times a week, and unless the bath is used every day, a change of under garments is necessary every 24 hours to be clean and comfortable. You will soon see this item of washing and ironing is no small thing in housekeeping in Florida, and it requires perhaps more clothing here than it does where the seasons are not so warm for the reason that the frequent washings and rough handling wears them out more than the actual wear I will close this article by advising all families who intend coming here to remain for some time to bring the help needed around the house, with them and be independent of the natives and negroes. Your outside work you can get done at much more reasonable prices.

SOMETHING ABOUT THE COST OF CLEANING, AND PREPARING LAND FOR ORANGE GROVES, AND TRUCK FARMS IN FLORIDA.

Suppose you purchase first quality high land usually covered with a thick growth of yellow pine trees; these must be removed, and a contract is made to clear the land and prepare it for the plow ; this will cost from 25 to 50 dollars per acre depending on whether the stumps are all to be taken out, and also the number of trees on an acre, and still more on the amount of grubbing. Should there be much saw palmetto(not usually the case on such land) on the land, the timber is worth something provided it is near a saw mill, then arrangements can be made to sell the timber on the stump or for a certain per cent after it is sawed. The best plan is to sell the stumpage, count the saw trees and get the money before the trees are cut, for should you agree on a per cent, it is advisable to remain with the saw mill party. In any case the clearing of the land will cost about the same, especially if the stumps must be removed which is difficult after the trees are off. The stumps are removed as follows : The sand is removed from around the roots to the depth of 12 or 15 inches, the roots are then chopped off and the tree in falling often draws out the tap root, otherwise it is cut off about a foot below the surface of the ground, the sand filled in, the roots covered, and as pine roots or stumps never sprout they are out of the way for all time to come. You now see that it is easier to remove the stumps while the tree stands, as it helps to pull its own stump, otherwise it must be dug out or cut so low as to be out of the way of the plow. The plowing will cost from 3 to 5 dollars per acre, fencing from .15 to $2.00 per rod depending on the kind

of fence.   The land after being grubbed and plowed should remain without planting for at least one
season, otherwise it will not produce it being wild
and sour, unless you stir (plow) it and use fertilizer. You must fertilize nearly all the time to grow
anything.   To plant an orange grove, here again
the cost is governed by the kind of trees planted.
Good thrifty budded trees three or four years old,
will cost you about one dollar each ; you can, however, get trees as low down in price as twenty-five
cents a piece that do sometimes make bearing trees
in the future.   Fifty orange trees to the acre is
about the right amount to plant, although some
plant as many as one hundred trees to the acre.
An orange tree should have about as much space
of ground to grow on as an apple tree in the
North.

Clearing second-class pine land usually costs
more than first-class, for the reason that there is
always more palmetto on it, although not nearly
so much timber.   The grubbing out of the palmetto
root is quite a job.   The tops are not large, being
only a bunch of leaves, but the stems of these leaves
are from a foot to four feet long, and some of them
are more than an inch through ; the shape or form
of the stem is about half round, having two sharp
edges, and the edges are full of teeth the entire
length, something like saw teeth, and are about
one-eighth of an inch long and sharp pointed and
about as close together as a number twelve saw

teeth; the points all turn toward the ground or butt of the stem and are hard and solid as a green briar and cut equally as badly when you come into contact with them. The roots of the saw palmetto do not lie deeply in the ground, that is the main or principal root; they, however, have small lateral roots that penetrate the ground to a considerable depth. The length and thickness of the main root are simply enormous; the fact is, it is hard to find the farther end of them and if it were not that they are not entirely underground, you could not find them at all. they extend for rods and rods, overlapping and intertwining with, and over each other thus completely covering the ground, in many places. They are of a kind of fibrous composition and are laminated, or grow in layers and between each layer is a kind of natural cloth that can be separated into sheets after the manner of isinglass, and after being separated, it has the appearance of having been woven in a loom; the warp and woof, or chain and filling are just as plainly shown as in a piece of burlap bagging. The writer has seen pieces of this stuff or natural cloth over a foot square; the leaf sowewhat resembles the palm leaf fan, so common in the North, but is solid only one-third of its length.

When you come to grubbing out this kind of stuff and making the land or sand tillable, it will cost you from thirty to eighty dollars per acre, especially should it be intermixed, which is very often the case with hog or scrub palmetto. The tops of this kind look like the saw palmetto, but it is much smaller in the top and teeth, the roots grow straight down like a beet and are from three to six inches in diameter, and from one to three feet long; they are much harder to grub out than the other kind.

FENCING, PLOUGHING, &C., SAME AS BEFORE STATED.

Hammock land is much harder to clear and prepare for a crop or a grove, and will cost more than double as much as any other kind of land to clear and prepare for the plow. After being once ready to plant, the expense for fertilizer is not by one-half as much as the pine lands; the cost of fencing, ploughing, planting, &c., is about the same in all cases.

The work of cleaning up land here is very laborious, and but few white men can stand it, or are able to perform that kind of labor, especially in the summer season, and the negroes work so slowly that it almost makes even a lazy white man tired to look at them working. You see by this description that the cost of building a new orange grove is quite an item, and particularly so, should it be a large one. After it is started, about the same attention must be given it as a field of corn in the North, and that continually for from seven to ten years before you begin to get returns worth speaking of. In addition you must spend for fertilizer.

on each tree, from twenty-five cents to a dollar per year, depending on the quality of soil it is planted on. True, in the meantime vegetables and garden truck can be raised at the same time after the first year, provided the right kind of fertilizer is used. In another part of this book you have learned something about the cost of raising vegetables in this sunny climate, and let me say that what is said about raising vegetable and all the other things written in this book is true. Interested persons, newspapers, circulars and other stories to the contrary, notwithstanding, and proper investigation and unbiased examination will amply prove the truth of the assertion. I will now give you an extract from a Florida newspaper, headed

DOES ORANGE CULTURE PAY?

"This is a question which many growers have been asking themselves. During the current season of depression in the business, a gentleman in Manatee county, whose name for the present we withhold, has kept books on this branch of Florida farming, and sends us the result, which, in his opinion, does not militate in favor of the grove. His account is kept with a five acre grove on good land, under most favorable circumstances with best attention. Here is the balance sheet after thirteen years of work:

ORANGE GROVE, DR.

To first cost near a railroad and growing town 5 acres at $50 per acre,	$ 250	00
To cost of clearing land, grubbing, felling timber, removing stumps, plowing and clearing,	250	00
To fencing, hog proof,	150	00
" 300 trees and setting same,	100	00
" cultivating trees ten years, man and horse		

half time, ploughing, hoeing. hauling fertilizer and applying, repairing fence, trimming, etc., $1.50 per pear,   1500 00

To horse in hauling, ploughing, etc, one half time,   900 00

To cost of fertilizer, average 10 cents to tree, 300 pounds a year, 10 years 30.000 pounds say $20 per ton,   300 00

To repairing fence estimate,   25 00

" interest on capital average of $1500,00 for ten years,   900 00

To use of land ten years for vegetable culture and other purposes, worth $100 per acre per year, being for five acres for ten years,   5000 00

To additional labor, double after ten years and double amount of fertilizer up to thirteenth year, man and horse three years $1000,00, fertilize. $100,   1100 00

Total cost and outlay at end of 13th year $10175 00

ORANGE GROVE, CR.

By yield 8th year, estimate to average to tree, total 30,000 at $5 00,   150 00

By yield 9th year double,   300 00

" " 10th " "   600 00

" " 11th " "   1200 00

" " 12th " "   2400 00

" " 13th " "   4800 00

" possible yield of vegetables for three years, average half crop among the trees, $50 per acre,   750 00

Total income, $10200 00

So that at the end of the thirteenth year under the most favorable circumstances, a man has barely got his money back. Under unfavorable circumstances, trees are so set back by the cold, drought, disease and insect life that at the end of ten years are not bearing, or at the end of the fifteenth year they do not bear, and time and money are thrown away.

I see many instances of this kind The readers can study the above balance sheet and draw their own conclusions."

POPULATION.

This is one of the things that there is no certainty about. You go into any small place in the State, ask how many inhabitants are in the place and nearly every one asked gives a different amount. Each town or city wants to be as big if not bigger than the other town, and my opinion is that were you to go to each town and city in the State and take the biggest figures that are given of each place, say nothing of the rural districts, as few people live there and add them together, you probably would have six or eight million inhabitants in the State, but when we come to solid facts, the census of 1880 gives as the population of the State (269,493) two hundred and sixty-nine thousand four hundred and ninety-three. The population has no doubt increased some in the last five or six years, but not to any great extent, so you perceive that there is not such a tremendous amount of people in Florida as many interested parties would have you believe.

TOURIST OR TRAVELLERS

Usually start at Jacksonville, goes up the St. Johns River to Sanford, then by the South Florida Railroad to Tampa, then to Charlotte Harbor or Cedar Keys by way of the Gulf of Mexico and then by the F. R. & N. C. Railroads to Gainesville, to Ocala, Silver Springs, Leesburg, Eustis, Tavares, Baldwin and Calahan, then returns to Jacksonville. Sometimes they take time to run up

to St. Augustine, then they, in their judgement or
estimation, have seen about all of Florida, and form
their conclusions accordingly, when in fact they
have seen and know but little about it. Your trip
up the river gives you the idea that Florida is little
else than marsh, water and low lands. At a few
places you get glimpses of the country, but most of
it is vast stretches of swamp land, cypress swamps,
cabbage palmetto, live oak, magnolia, pine trees
and black murky water, for the St. Johns River is
by no means a clear water stream, though I recon
no person ever saw its waters muddy; then at Sanford, you board the train and until you arrive at
Winter Park and Orlando you pass through a
sandy country that to Northern eyes, does not seem
to be good for much, and I am not sure but the
ideas then formed, are very nearly correct; then
from Orlando until you arrive at Kissimmee, the
most of the land is flat pine woods and unless in
a dry time, most of it is under water, notwithstanding all this, some of the very best lands in the
State, are right here in the neighborhood of Kissimmee City, but you run right on to Bartow, and
here you will find a superabundance of sand that
will not impress you very favorably, and away you
go to Tampa or to Charlotte Harbor—it is still
sand. You ask the price of land here and the figures will be such as to make you open your eyes in
amazement, and you will surely think the parties
are jesting, but on further inquiry you will find it

is reality. and if you wish to own any real estate composed of sand in that neighborhood, you will have to come down with the cash to the amount of the price asked, or some other man will own it while you are thinking about the trade; you cannot see (or any person else for that matter) what in the world makes this land so valuable; you soon get disgusted with the place and leave for Cedar Keys. This place you have heard and read about and the chances are that when you get there, you will be so much disappointed that you will not even ask the price of real estate at all, but will leave by the first train for Gainesville. Here you will probably be disappointed, too, but it will be the other way; the place being so much better than expected; I do not mean the land, for that is still sand, but the buildings and the enterprise and business of the town. It is more like a Northern town than any one I have seen in the State. The town is well laid off, the streets are wide and good board and brick pavements are laid all over the business part of the town, as well as on many of the streets where the private residences are, and many of the buildings are of brick and well built; you will also find that property here is held at very high figures, so that a man of ordinary means must look elsewhere. From here you will go to Waldo. Here is said to be the largest orange tree in the State, which is said to have yielded at a single crop as many as thirty thousand oranges. About this time you will be about ready to return to Jacksonville, or it may be you will visit Silver Springs, Ocala and some other places, but in any event you will soon return to the starting point. After a review of the trip, you will possibly begin to think that there is either not much in this Florida business or that you have made a mistake in the route taken. You did make a mistake in the route, and as for there not being much in it, you may be more than half right in that also.

On your first arrival at Jacksonville you should have gone direct to Gainesville by rail, then either bought or hired a horse and buggy there, got some man (and there are plenty of them to be had by simply bearing their expenses) that was well acquainted with the country, and then drove about the county, gradually working Southward by way of Orange Lake, Citra, Micanopy. Ocala, Wier Lake. Leesburg, Eustis, Maitland, Tavares. Apopka, Ocoee, Gotha, Lake Butler, and so on as long as your inclination and time would allow and your money in your purse held out, in the meantime talking to everybody and anybody that will talk to you, ask all the questions you can think of and ask the same questions of different persons, and do not pass the negroes by, they very often can, and will give you information that is obtainable in no other way. A sojourn in the State of two or three months in this way will give you more minute and correct information concerning the ins and outs, advantages and disadvantages of it than you could obtain in any other way in double or even quadruple the time, in fact there is no other way to find out all about Florida and the people of the State, but to go there and mingle with them, and as to safety of a persons life and property, you are just as safe in almost any part of Florida, (if you conduct yourself properly) as you would be anywhere else in the United States, and a great deal safer than many places I know of that boast of their high state of morality and civilization.

ACCLIMATATION.

Persons may come to Florida in the late fall season and remain until early spring and escape any and all bad effects from change of climate, or sometimes they can take a tour of a month or two at almost any season or time of the year, and not feel any change so far as their bodily condition is concerned, but to come and remain here for a year or more, your system will, and must undergo a climatic change, and this change usually shows itself by affecting the bowels and sometimes very seriously, or by a spell of a kind of low type of fever or by sores and boils, particularly on the ankles and legs and by the sand or Florida itch, which it will be almost miraculous should you escape the latter. Should you remain in the State a whole year at one time, this acclimatation, while it seldomproves fatal, is very annoying. A little

pimple with a yellow spot or head will rise, say on
your ankle or somewhere between the ankle and
the knee; it is a small bit of a sore not worth mind-
ing at first, but in a day or two it inflames and enlarges so that in a very short space of time it is an
open sore that you could not cover with a silver
dollar, and if the proper remedies are not applied,
it will extend all around the leg, and perhaps you
will not get this sore healed until another one
starts on the other leg or on your arm, and frequently these sores are on both legs and arms at
the same time. It is very seldom that any sores of
this kind break out on the body, but the body is
the place for the sand itch. Should you have a
spell of sickness soon after arriving here, you will
probably escape the sores, but not one in ten escapes
the itch. You cannot imagine how annoying it is
to have to rub or scratch, and the more you scratch
the more itchy the parts become; you become almost wild, and I recon that if ever you felt like
saying *cuss words*, you will feel like it about this
time. Well, let me tell you, that if you come to
Florida to live and you stay here, you will in all
human probability go through this ordeal. It is
an axiom and self-evident that in changing from
one climate to another, where the living is different, what you eat is different, your habits must
change with the country—almost everything is
changed, and consequently your system must
change to conform to the climate; this, then is b,-

coming acclimated, and it is a law of nature that must, and will be obeyed, you, however, by proper care in eating, do not overindulge in anything, expose yourself as little as possible to the direct rays of the sun, remain indoors in the heat of the day, and by observing natures laws carefully and closely, you will thus become acclimated without any serious trouble to yourself or any person else.

WHO SHOULD GO TO OR VISIT FLORIDA.

All persons who have an abundance of money, and who make a business of spending their summers at Northern watering places, such as Saratoga, White Mountains, Deer Park, Ocean Grove, and other such places in order to spend their money avoid the extreme heat of summer and thus enjoy life by going to Florida and spending the winter season. There you will avoid the extreme cold and freezing winters of the North, and can bask in the sunshine of Florida to your hearts content, and have all the out and indoor enjoyment you want, provided you have plenty of money.

Florida in the true sense of the word, is a winter resort and that is about all it is. You now perceive that the pleasure seekers should all come here in the winter season.

HUNTING AND FISHING.

The parties who delight in hunting and fishing, and who care nothing for time or much how they live, should come here and have a good time generally, as game and particularly fish, in many parts

are plenty and with a little manoeuvering and exertion, game and fish enough, with pelts and alligator hides, can be caught and sold to keep soul
and body together. I know of no place that would
suit people of the above class any better than in
Florida.

SPECULATORS.

The parties who make a business of speculating
in a business way in lands in towns and lots, can
find no better field to ply their vocation in, provided they have money to pay as they go, they will
make money rapidly, provided their judgement is
good and properly exercised.

Sick and feeble persons who are afflicted with
asthmatic and pulmonary troubles are often benefited and sometimes entirely cured by spending
their winters in Florida, provided they come here
before the disease becomes too deeply seated. The
trouble with this class of people is that they try all
the home remedies that they can get hold of before
coming here, and by this time it is very often too
late, and the climate of Florida or any other climate will not do them any good. If you come at
all, come when the disease is in its first stages,
otherwise you had better stay at home. Every
person that has the time and money to spend should
take a trip to Florida and then they will know
something about it and can judge for themselves
about what kind of a place it is and what kind of a
climate it has.

TIME TO COME.

This depends a good deal on what you are going to Florida for. If on a tour or visit, one time is as good as another—I would say come whenever you please. If, however, to remain in Florida a year or more, come in the fall, either in October or November for the reason that the acclimating process (which all who come here from a distance and remain here must expect to go through) will be likely to affect you much less severely than at any other time ; let me here say, if you think of becoming a citizen of Florida, whether you have a family or not by all manner of means go and see it and remain until satisfied that it is a better place than where you now are, and then move there and not until then. Should you find or think Florida not the place, then remain at the present location, or seek a home elsewhere.

WHO SHOULD NOT COME TO FLORIDA

Except to see it. Persons who are well situated in the North, or who are in moderate circumstances having a comfortable home, and doing well enough had better let well enough alone. The mechanic who can make a living in the North, cannot better his condition here for the reason that wages are no better than where he is. The clerk has no business here at all except in isolated cases for the reason that hundreds of men in delicate health come to Florida for their health, who not having a superabundance of *lucre*, attempt to help out same by clerking or any light work they can find. Many of them will work or clerk for their boarding and even less, as whatever they do make or get, is that much ahead. Many of them are first-class clerks, so you see there is no use of clerks, and they should not come, if to better their conditions be the object.

SCHOOL TEACHERS.

School teachers get better wages in almost any other State than Florida, yet there are some good schools here and the people brag considerably about their educational institutions.

DAY LABORERS.

Day laborers need not be idle here unless they want to ; wages, however, are no better for general work than they are in the North. About the only advantage a day laborer has, he need not lose much time by reason of snows and bad weather, and if he can stand the heat, he might do about as well here as elsewhere, but no better.

SICKLY PERSONS.

Especially if much reduced by reason of sickness except as before stated, should not come here, for the change will be more likely to do harm than good, particularly if the person has not an abundance of money, for they will find that the cost of comfortable living is high, and as the worry on account of the expense of living and enormous bills that the doctors will charge, will, in all probability aggravate the disease and make it worse instead of better, and here an idea occurs to me that if your family physician, who knows all about your system and has had a chance to note all the symptoms and facts connected therewith, cannot do you any good. It does seem to me to be the heighth of folly to suppose for a moment that a strange doctor who knows nothing at all about you or your case, should be able to do you much, if any good, so in my judgement you had better remain at home and save your time and money.

THE LAZY MAN.

The lazy man will find his business entirely over-done all through the State, and will find no open-ings to pursue his calling. There are most too many lazy people here now, both male and female

MERCHANDISING.

The handling of dry goods, groceries, boots and shoes and indeed all kinds of merchandising is overdone in all parts of the State that I have been in or can hear of. The general complaint is, that there are more stores than the place affords, conse-quently the merchant need not come here expect-ing to make a big fortune at the business, and if he does come in the face of all this, he will in the end, in nine cases out of ten reap disappointment and loss.

STOCK RAISING.

In some parts of the State, particularly in the extreme Southern counties, there are large cattle ranches, and certain parties make a business of raising cattle. There are parties who own from a few hundred head to many thousands. I suppose this is so, because a number of people say it is so. These cattle have no special care, but run at large the whole year around; at certain times in the year, these cattle are, what is called rounded up, coralled and branded. Each owner has a brand peculiarly his own. This brand is recorded in the archives of the State and all cows (cattle) having this brand, belongs to the party owning said brand. No two brands dare, or can be alike.

The native cattle or cows of Florida are all small, the best of them being not much better than a good yearling calf at the North.

In the winter season the cattle become poor; during the late summer and fall they are in much better condition. The best of these cattle are selected out, gathered up and driven Northward in the State until the owner finds a market for them. They usually have from thirty to fifty in a bunch, and sell them to butchers, who cuts them out, (as they call butchering here). These cows sell for, from five to ten dollars a head, depending more on age than quality. You observe that this sandy country and warm climate does not produce either large or fat cattle, nor do they bring big prices, and yet they bring all they are worth, because they are not worth more than they bring. Often the beef in the markets here is something like this; Take a poor steer or cow from among the poorest stock cattle you can find in the North, kill and cut up, and you have something a good deal like the Florida beef, especially that which is killed here during the winter and early spring. As befors stated the cattle are in much better condition in summer and fall, consequently the beef is better, but Florida beef at its best, would be considered sorry stuff in the North, and so it is in Florida.

The Florida pork is better than the beef, particularly so when the hogs are penned; when they are left run at large, the meat is a kind of a reddish yellow color. This is caused by by the hogs eating what is called paint root, which grows wild in this country. This paint root grows something like the artichoke of the North; the roots are small and seem to be much hunted, after by the wild hogs, which devour them greedily with the above result to the meat. It is said the meat is perfectly healthy; it may be, I want but little of it in mine. The native hog when full grown and in ordinary case, will average in weight about fifty pounds. It is a very large one indeed, and very fat, that will weigh one hundred pounds. There are a number of hogs running wild in the wild lands of Florida. These are common property, but are generally so gaunt and wild that they are about as hard to shoot as deer, or any other wild game, and after you have them, they are not of much account.

An extract from the Times Union, a daily paper

published at Jacksonville, Florida, in their issue of Sept. 4th, containing the following on stock raising :

"Stock raising in Florida is much discussed in the newspapers and in private circles, but upon few subjects so much discussed is there manifest so great degree of ignorance of the merits of the question.

The climate condition of the country, the varieties of vegetation, the drouths that some seasons prevail, and rains at others, covering the entire surface with water for miles in extent; the flies that goad the cattle to frenzy at times, and rob them of their life blood; the need of proper food at some seasons, and not least the fact that the Southern cattle fever is endemic in all portions of the State, and particularly in the South, a disease that all cattle in this State at some period of their lives must undergo, and which in one-half the cases terminate fatally with imported cattle and thus preventing breeding up from imported blood, are seldom or never taken into account by those who have acquired their experience in stock raising in other States, and especially in the great plains of the west. There, each blade that springs from the soil, is as nutritious as the blue grass of Kentucky, or the white clover of the Northern pastures, and when the rains have ceased and the frosts have come, its nutriment is not dissipated, but parched and dried, still give food to the flocks and herds, but in Florida not more than three-fifths of what grows in the water-soaked ground, contains any nutriment, and if we are to give credit to the actions of the men who have the care of Florida cattle, the dried vegetables are only fit to light the flames that strip the whole regions of their summer growths.

On the plaines and in the pastures of the Northern States cattle can find dry beds on which to repose and ruminate, but in Florida there occur seasons when the cattle would need to travel miles to find a dry spot on which to lie, and then herders are often compelled to make their bed on a fallen log or upon a pile of bushes and grass, where they may secure such sleep as they can in the midst of swarms of mosquitoes and flies.

These lands may answer for cattle pasture during the dry season; for there does come times when it may require as many miles to find water for drinking, as in the wet seasons to secure the dry place for the stock to lie upon. Every stockman must admit that dry land on which the cattle may lie, as well as easy access to water for drinking purposes, are absolute necessities for the health of stock. If our position on this point be correct and the character of the country, such as those who have ridden over many miles of it describe it, then it follows that this is not a stock region of great value. It might be used advantageously in connection with dry lands to which the cattle might retreat for resting places; and it may be drained of its covering of water. (If a place can be found to drain it into.) The noxious vegetation destroyed and the more nutritious grasses, like Bermuda para and smutt grasses introduced, and thus become as famous for its grazing qualities as for its genial climate, but in its present condition, it is very different from the dry plains, mountain sides and valleys of the great west, and men should not allow themselves to be deceived by appearances during such dry seasons as have been during the past two or three years, or by the flattering accounts of land agents, whose objects are to secure a commission for selling.

Cattle raising in Florida may, and should be prominently adjunctive to a more general farming, but from the natural conditions of Florida, it will scarcely reach the position of a leading industry, far less will it ever become the leading staple product."

HORSES.

As before stated are small and will not average in weight much over 600 pounds, but are quite hardy and can stand more work than the general run of horse flesh, gentle and docile and do not seem to be vicious or to have bad habits although tricks will be learned if not properly handled.

From what has been written it will be seen that all the domestic animals of Florida are small, some indeed quite small, and little effort is made to improve the domestic stock; the little effort that has been made resulted in failure. A few good bulls have been brought into the State and turned with the herds, and that was the last heard of the imported bulls. The forage and climate does not

seem to agree with other than the native cattle nor
do I have an idea that the bovines and equines of
Florida can be much improved until Florida becomes an agricultural country where all the cereals
and tame grasses can be grown, and this according to the present nature and climate of the State
will never be.

And now let us ask why it is that Florida is such
a great place.   If it is as so often represented, why
is it that the horses, cattle, hogs, and many of the
wild animals are so small and insignificant? and
why is it that even with all the fertilizing that can
be done, there is no extra or even large vegetables
of any kind grown in the State? but on the contrary, the vegetables and nearly everything that
grows out of the ground are of only ordinary or
inferior size as compared with the same vegetables
and other things in the countries or places in which
the same vegetables and things grow and mature.
This subject of size and maturity of vegetables, etc,
is a subject that should not be overlooked by persons or parties emigrating from one place to another.   There certainly is something in it and another thing you will see by observing closely, that
in all the blowing and booming that interested
parties give to Florida, there is very little said
about size and quality, it is all quantity. The
reason of this is that size and quality (oranges and
a few other things excepted,) will not bear investigation, therefore they are left in the background.
The quantity misleads, and you take for granted

when the quantity is sufficient, it is understood that
size and quality must, or at least ought to corres-
pond ; take for example : Mr. John S—— has
ten thousand head of fat cattle—this is quantity , you at once conclude that these cattle are
large and in first-class condition—this is size and
quality. Now this conclusion is legitimate and
natural, and one that almost any man would arrive
at under ordinary conditions, but as before stated
in this book, Florida has a climate and also many
other conditions peculiarly her own, and these must
all be well understood to arrive at true conclusions.
I have described the size of cattle in Florida as
well as what the people there call fat beef; now
you see that size and quality has a different meaning than that conveyed in the notice that Mr. John
S—— had ten thousand head of cattle. This
same comparison or explanation will carry out in
nearly all cases where quantity is spoken of, and
you will in a very large majority of the cases find
size and quality very conspicuous on account of,
or by reason of ther absence in their description.

Another thing the people in the North are led to
believe and that is that in Florida the people always have an abundance of fresh vegetables, such
as radishes, lettuce, spinach, beans, peas, tomatoes,
cucumbers, squashes, red beets, melons, turnips,
and indeed all kinds of garden sass, the whole
year around ; that all that is to be done is to go into the garden-patch and get whatever you want

and whenever you need it, and also bring right along a basket of strawberries, a pine apple or a bunch of bananas, figs or pomegranates, oranges or some other tropical fruit. Such, however, is not the case by any manner or of means, all garden truck, vegetables and fruit have their seasons and while this season is perhaps a little longer and comes much earlier than in the North, the rotation is very similar to the same products in the North. All vegetables and seeds that are usually planted in the North in April and May, in this country to make a crop, must be planted in January and February; if planted here much later the hot sun and dry weather prevents their maturing. It is true, however, that if you plant in the month of November and get no frost in December and January, (nearly always frosts in both these months all over Florida,) you will sometimes get a few vegetables as a kind of second crop. I have ate watermelons in November taken right from the vine : this, however is the exception, and not the rule. After July, and I may say after June, the vegetable crop in Florida is over until the following March or April. Do not understand that we do not have any vegetable and tubers in Florida during all these months from July to March, for we do have them, but very much the larger part of them are shipped into the State from other places, but the strong probability s that, unless you have plenty of money at command, you will not indulge much in eating them.

When Irish potatoes are a dollar a peck, as they
now are, July 2d, 1886, it is not likely that people
in ordinary circumstances wil indulge very extravagantly or extensively in them. Apples, peaches,
pears, plums, cherries, grapes, currants, rasp-
berries, blackberries, gooseberries, and all such
fruits and berries are seldom seen anywhere in
Florida, except in the large towns and then the
price is such as to be only within the reach of comparatively few of the inhabitants. The above
named fruits and berries, however can be had almost any place in the State in the form of canned
goods at tolerably reasonable prices, considering
you are a long way or distance from where they
grow. The facts are that Florida is not now, and
in my judgement never will be self-supporting.
If it were not that Northern capital is largely invested in speculative enterprises, there would be
very little, if any money afloat. Speculation you
know is no producer ; (Its plain name is gamb-
ling), and the money made by speculation does
not by any means, enhance the producing qualities
of the country, but rather retards the progress of
any country or town ; take for example a town anywhere that is just newly laid out and is just fairly
started. Capitalists come along and buy a number of lots in what should be the business part of
the town ; it may be under a verbal promise that he
will build and improve so and so, thus he is en-
abled to get the lots at a low figure, but as soon as

he has the deeds for the lots, he now says, gentle-
men these lots are mine, and if any person wants
them, they can have them at about so much; he
will put his figures at double or treble what he paid
for them. If parties do not want them at these
figures, the lots are put into the hands of an agent
and off the owner goes, regular dog in the manger
style, he will neither improve or allow any person
else to do so unless he doubles his money. Now
his buying these lots does not enhance the producing qualities of these lots one iota, but his buying them on speculation has undoubtedly retarded
the progress of the town sometimes to that degree
that persons who would buy and build, go elsewhere and invest their money where speculation
does not run quite so high. Many cases of this
kind have come under the writers observation down
here in this "sunny climate," but what causes this
speculation? The plain answer is this! Booming,
lying and misrepresentation, for there is nothing
substantial to back up the State, no production
that will, or ever can be made to pay in any shape
or form whatever as a general crop, and there is
nothing to export from the State that will bring a
revenue. There is not much over a quarter of a
million of inhabitants in the State, and the State in
itself cannot begin to support what are now here
and if you take out of it all the speculating capital
and the produce and stuff that is shipped in from
the North and elsewhere, nine-tenths of all her in-

habitants would be obliged to go somewhere else; for it would be impossible for them to obtain a living in her borders. I am well satisfied from personal observance that there is in value shipped into the State at least ten dollars to every one that is shipped out of it of its own production. This, no doubt will seem strange to some of my readers who have read of the wonderful productions of this wonderful State of Florida, but no matter how strange and startling it may appear, when you come to investigate this matter closely, you will find the facts as set forth in this book, to be about the true state of the case. I will only say in

CONCLUSION

That all persons who have a desire to come to Florida may come, the road is open and it does not cost much to get here, but look out after you do get here, but let me advise all who do come to see well to it that you are not misled. Get all the information you can from every source and from personal inspection and investigation, then make up your minds either to come or stay where you are. Should you come and succeed well, if you do not succeed well, you will have to blame somebody other than the writer, for if, after having carefully read this little book you are still in the dark, then nothing but sad experience will enlighten you.

And now the writers task is finished; how well it is done is for the reader to judge, and for the visitor, tourist and emigrant to Florida to know;

especially the latter. The book is not written in high flown language or filled with rounded periorations, the aim has been to write so that any, and all who read this book will, or can understand it. Some parts seem to be tautological; this the writer deemed necessary to the proper and full understanding of these particular parts. Again the writer is wholly responsible for the entire work, except parts of two letters quoted or copied and the balance sheet on orange grove. The writer has written entirely from personal knowledge, observation and his own judgement, being right on the ground while writing, and the object of the book is the greatest good to the greatest number, and if what is said herein written is heeded as it should be, then the object will be accomplished.

Moreover the writer is well aware of the fact that land agents, land sharks, speculators and parties who are interested in the sale of Florida lands (sand), but who in few instances live or make their homes there (the whole year around), but who do make their money there, will deny the facts set forth in this book, and will no doubt say all manner of things about the writer, and will cry out, "Great is the Goddess Diana of the Epheseans" because their shrines and craft is endangered. Reader make the application yourself. But be it known, the writer owes no man in Florida anything and he has no favors to ask, or is he much afraid of any person face to face. He has been, and lived in a good many of these United States. He has always tried to live as closely to the "golden rule" as possible. He has lived long enough in Florida to know that what is written in this book is about as near the facts as they can be put on paper, and he further knows that a residence of a year or two in the State, will demonstrate the truth too late however, for this book to do the demonstrator or experimenter any good, only he will then know if he had given proper attention to what was written in the book, he would have saved time, money and perhaps health; such is "Florida as it is." THE AUTHOR.

APPENDIX.

Dogs, cats, hogs, and nearly all domestic and wild animals are polluted with mites. These mites look just like small fleas. They are black in color, very active—jump like fleas, are very hard to catch; they get on the human body whenever opportunity offers, and sometimes when it does not offer, and when they do get on you, you will think from their bite and other movements that they are fleas— and they are fleas, and of the worst kind at that, but they are mites in Florida. These mites or fleas (not chicken lice) that get on domestic fowls, are of a different species, they have the appearance of those above described only much smaller. This kind, it is said will not stay on the human body (I doubt this, however.) They become so numerous on the fowls at certain times, that unless destroyed by proper remedies, they literally destroy the skin and the fowls will die. It is said the same remedies that destroy chicken lice will also destroy these chicken fleas.

As before noted, the buzzards are numerous here, and they are all polluted with mites. This is no doubt true, from the fact that if you be to a slaughter pen where buzzards gather very thickly, they being after the beef of-fall, &c , soon after they have been there, and in a short time you will find yourself polluted with mites, and these mites are identical with chicken lice. All, or nearly all the wild beasts, and especially the plume birds, herrons, cranes, and such as are so much sought after, killed and dressed for ladies headgear, are literally polluted with these abominable mites and fleas and I sometimes think if the ladies knew what kind of messes they wore on their headgear, these plumes would not be quite so highly prized, but human nature is pretty nearly the same all over, and one-half the world does not know, or do they care much what the other half eats or wears, only so they get the money for it.

As to the cattle (cows), I do not know, or could I by any means find out whether or no they were or are infested with fleas, but they are infested with ticks, a kind of a large louse. I have seen some of these ticks when they had sucked themselves full of blood that were as large as a small hickory nut; the usual size of this kind of tick is about the size of a large sheep louse. There is also another species of tick called a seed tick; this one is very minute and are plenty They are a wee mite larger than the red bug, but they do not seem to be as poisonous as the red bug, but are nearly as annoying when they get on you. They are black and can be seen with the naked eye, even before they have filled themselves; when they are full they drop off and wait for the next victim, whether it be man or beast, they do not appear to have any particular choice on whom or what they prey.

As to human body, lice or gray backs I know nothing about them, never having seen one in all my life, but I rather suppose they are in Florida also, for nearly all the little pests I know of or have ever heard of, are here, and it is not very likely that the graybacks are missing. As to ants, they are here of all sizes, from the tiny little red fellows to the big winged one that is an inch and a quarter long, and of all the known species or sorts that are in the United States. There is a red ant that is about one quarter of an inch long that gets into the houses same as the little red ones. These are very destructive and pugnacious, and when they get on your person as they frequently do, they bite or pinch furiously.

About stinging insects. These are not more numerous than in some other parts. I now speak of these insects that have stings in the business end. We have a few bumble bees, hornets, yellow jackets, wasps and a few other stinging insects There is also a good many scorpions; this is something apparently between a small sized lizard and a large spider and has a sting in its tail and is very poisonous and dangerous.

About flies: House or common flies are about as they are elsewhere; where much filth is they are plenty, otherwise not so numerous, there are however, very many more of the large grayish or blue flies here than I ever saw anywhere else; there are several species of large flies known as clags, that are among cattle and horses of a species that I never saw only here; there are several species of what are called mosquito and fly wasps that seem to destroy the flies to some considerable extent: sometimes if you are near a herd or bunch of cattle, you will hear a noise something like bees swarming and you will see thousands of these wasps all over and among the cattle: The cattle do not seem to mind them at all, and on close watching you will see these wasps catching flies. As soon as a wasp catches a fly, he makes a bee line for somewhere; where it goes, or what it does with the fly I do not know. What are called in the North snake sarvers or snake feeders, are called mosquito wasps. These mosquito wasps are numerous and so are the mosquitoes, and right here I would say that either the mosquito wasps do not understand their business, or that there are not enough of them to do the business, for there is a very large superabundance of mosquitos left over and above what are destroyed by the wasps, if they destroy them at all. Worms of all kinds except angle worms, are very numerous. It is almost impossible to keep anything in the shape of dried fruits or berries. these little crawling pests get into them and destroy them. Yeast or yeast cakes may be good when you get or buy them, but in a few days are full of worms; flour and corn meal in a very short time is literally crawling with worms; spices and even black pepper and tobacco becomes wormy—the latter two may seem uncreditable, I did not believe it until I saw it myself. It is impossible to keep fresh meats of any kind over twelve hours, and I have seen it swarming with maggots in less than six hours from the time it was killed; without iee and plenty of ice at that, and the best refrigerators will not keep fresh meets sweet and good without turning green much over forty-eight hours, although many butchers and others do keep and sell it. After the expiration of the above mentioned time, how good or healthy it is, I will leave for you to judge. The fact is, if the people who visit Florida knew exactly in what condition many of the things they are eating had been, they would turn from them in disgust. A whole chapter might be written on how butchers, and particularly hotel and boarding house keepers prepare their meats for sale and table, but I will dismiss the subject by simply saying that if it were not for charcoal, soda, smoke and spices, much meat that now goes into the human stomach would go into the buzzards craw.

An item on farming in Orange county, Florida. A few days ago the writer in conversation with a Florida farmer he said he owned a sixteen acre farm within two miles of a lively town of twelve hundred inhabitants, that eight acres were cleared and under the best of cultivation; it had all been cow-penned and well tramped, that he had quite a number of orange trees on it, some of which were in bearing; that part of it was in corn; that it was the best corn he had ever seen in Florida, (he lived in the State all his life) and he believed it would make nearly twenty bushels of corn to the acre; that his buildings were pretty fair log dwelling house and stables that besides this he had about seventy head of cattle (he said cows) from one to twenty years of age, ten or twelve head of hogs and a good many chickens; and that he wanted to sell the whole outfit; that he must have money, and would take thirteen hundred dollars for the whole business, real estate and all, and make a good and sufficient warrantee deed, and give possession at once. Now the writer knows all about this particular man and his place, and further that the man did not misrepresent anything, and the property seems to be cheap, and is cheap as a speculation, and I know that by a little booming in this case, a clear thousand dollars could be made inside of six months, yet with all this, I would not take the price asked and what could be made beside and be compelled to live on this place for two years. Now if you will read the above over again carefully, you can perhaps read between the lines a good deal more than what there is written on the lines, and perhaps get something that will engage your thinking powers for sometime, and in the end you will perhaps wonder what about the end man.

You no doubt frequently hear and read about the prairies of Florida: you who live in the North-West know what prairies are in that country, and form your conclusions at once that the Florida prairies are about the same. Again, when you come to see them, you will find out your mistake as in many other things. What they call prairies here, are well defined natural markings generally around cypress swamps, where neither trees or bushes grow, and it is covered with water about half the year. It only differs from Marsh lands in, that it is sandy bottom and nothing will grow on this kind of land but the poorest kind of grass and not very much of that. These so called prairies are from a few yards to several hundred yards wide, or in other words, they extend back from the cypress swamp until the land becomes high enough that the pine trees will grow. There is another kind of land that is sometimes called prairie, that is, when as is sometimes the case, a lake becomes dry from the bottom falling out or in some other way. See account of Lake Levy or Paines Prairie, This comes much nearer being a prairie, than anything they have in Florida, but the fact is there is no land in the State that I, or you either, for that matter would call prairie land by any means.

When you come to Florida, before you eat or sleep ascertain what it is going to cost you for a meal or a bed, otherwise you will probably think you have been overcharged. Again, if you have a trunk or anything to carry (haul), better make a bargain before the work is done, otherwise you will probably pay seventy-five cents where twenty-five cents should have paid the bill. So, in having any work done of any kind, mechanical or otherwise, have it well understood what you are to pay, either by the day or job, and if the amount is of any considerable size, have the contract in writing and well specified, otherwise you will, in all probability have to pay in the end from one-half to double as much more as was agreed upon for example the writer contracted (verbally) with a party to do a certain job of mechanical work, specifying by drawings how the work was to be done for a specified sum of money to be paid when the work was finished; all well the work was done, and not very well done either, the party refused to abide by his contract (there was no witness) and charged by the day, so that instead of the bill being one hundred and ten dollars, it was run up to within a few dollars of two hundred and there was no other way than to pay or have a law suit, which in Florida, above all other places, should, and must be avoided. Now, had the above verbal contract been in writing and well specified, the writer would have saved about seventy-five dollars, There was a small amount of extra work that should have been paid for, and it was mighty well paid for too.

Many more instances and examples could be given, particu-

larly in setting out groves, clearing up lands, etc., where the
absolute necessity of written contracts come in and without
them you will certainly get the worst of the bargain, and with
them the chances are about even to hold your own, and tight
match too.

And now should you ever visit Florida, and I hope you will
and give heed to the advice given, in a very short time it will
save you many times the price of this little book in this one
item alone.

UNDERWRITING OR FIRE INSURANCE

In Florida presents a rather singular and perplexing feature,
If the State is so prosperous, so healthy and such an excellent
place to do business in, why is it that nearly all the old reliable and substantial fire insurance companies, both in Europe
and America, refuse to do business in the State? Many of
these companies did start to do business in the State, but after
a trial of a year or two, on account of the enormous losses and
unprofitableness of the business, cancelled their policies and
withdrew from the State, and to-day there is no strong, reliable fire insurance company outside of the State or inside either, that I know of (and I have made dilligent inquiry) that
cares to, or will establish an agency in her borders, and those
that are now doing business in the State, are withdrawing
as fast as their licenses expire.

Rates of insurance against loss by fire in the State are enormously high, amounting in many cases to as much as ten per
cent per annum of the amount insured, and even with their
rates, nine-tenths of the companies that have done business in
the State in the last three years, have done it at a loss, in many
cases thousands of dollars annually. These facts are taken
from the State Treasurers report, who is also the insurance
commissioner by virtue of his office of Treasurer.

Now this state of things indicates and shows very clearly
that underwriting in the State of Florida is at present in no
flourishing condition. Referance being had to the above
named reports, will establish this fact beyond doubt or cavil.
I think I could give good reasons for this state of affairs, but
will let the readers draw their own inference and conclusions.

A TURPENTINE ORCHARD.

Consists of a pine forest of from ten to one hundred or more acres of heavily timbered yellow, or
terpentine pine land. The trees are kerfed or

chopped in from four to six inches deep, about two
feet from the ground the kerf is cut in the form of
a bowl, so that it will contain from two to four
quarts of liquid.   The kerf is cut about one-third
round the tree, the bark and white wood is then
hewn or chopped off above the kerf from four to
six feet, and little gutters cut lengthwise on this surface all leading into the bowl shaped kerf.   The
crude turpentine soon begins to flow or ooze out
of the surface and runs into the kerf from which it is
removed into buckets and barrels and taken to the
still where it undergoes the process of distillation.
RESULTANT, SPIRITS OF TURPENTINE
AND ROSIN.

When the trees are first tapped or prepared a
nearly pure liquid turpentine runs out, and in a few
days it begins to harden and forms a kind of a
crust on the out surface and in the kerf.   This
crust if left for several days becomes quite thick
and tough; this removed with scrapers and taken
to the still same as liquid and undergoes the same
process.   About once a month the trees are gone
over with an adze or ax and a little wood taken
off the turpentine surface.   The next season the
opposite side of tree is treated in the same way
with as good results; thus you see a turpentine
orchard is good for two years, though some parties cut the trees so as to make three turpentine
faces, then it takes three years to exhaust the timber.   The timber after being exhausted is used

for lumber, it being just as good as if the turpentine had not been drawn off except the few feet of each tree that had been hew nor hacked to obtain the turpentine and rosin.

The process of distilling turpentine is similar to distilling other substances, but is attended with a good deal of danger on account of its inflamable nature. It therefore requires a good deal of skill and care to run a turpentine still with safety and profit. There are but few turpentine stills in Florida, not because there is not plenty of the right kind of pine, but I think the reason is, there is too much work for the money made by the process.

A review of the Diston Land and Drainage Company's doings, written about the beginning of September, A. D., 1886, immediately after a rainy season of about ten weeks duration:

Sometime about the beginning of 1882 this company commenced operations on the banks of Lake Tohopekaliga, where the town of Kissimmee now stands, they built two small steam boats, the Okeechobee and the Rosalie, and several dredge boats, dug a canal four miles long at the South end of Lake Tohopekaliga. This canal seemed to lower the water in said lake several feet and a good deal of marsh land seemed to be in a fair way to become fit for cultivation. The company were encouraged by this seeming success and proceeded to cut a canal between East and West Tohopekaliga Lakes. When this canal was completed the effect was to lower the water in East Tohopekaliga some three or four feet, and the marshes thus drained have not been submerged since. The company then worked further South, opening up water ways so that at this date there is steam boat navigation and water communication through to the Gulf of Mexico. In the meantime the so-called reclaimed lands were largely advertised throughout the United States and Europe, and the strongest kind of inducements held out for the people to come and invest their money and settle upon these lands. Many persons did come, bought and settled and began making improvements some of them on a large scale, the land appearing all right, it being composed almost entirely of decayed vegetable matter, the accumulation of hundreds of years. As soon as the marshes became dry enough, they were cultivated, vegetables were planted and grew miraculously, the seasons continuing dry for several years, and everything works to advantage of the Company and to those who bought. Cabbage tomatoes, beans, Irish potatoes, cucumbers, melons &c., grew and produced immense crops. Pine apples. bananas, lemons, and even orange trees were planted and are doing well, when in January 1886 a cold snap came and froze the crops. The parties planted their crops again and grew rapidly and were harvested before the rainy season set in, the corn, sugar cane and later crops were in prime condition, when on the 19, of June 1886 it began to rain. In a short time the lakes filled up and the so-called reclaimed lands with their crops were covered with water. For some reason the canals failed to carry the water off and on Sept. 3, 1886, the waters in all the lakes and marshes south of the Tohopkaligas rose higher than before the Drainage Company commenced operations. The water in East Tohopkaliga did not rise within about three feet of where it was before being drained. West Tohopkaliga was advertised as being lowered six feet, but to-day its waters are about a foot of being as high as it was before the Company began work, leaving thousands of acres of corn and sugar cane submerged making a total loss as it has now been under water over two months and it rains almost every day. The waters in the south part of the State are said to be higher than for years, whether from cutting canals and partially draining the upper lakes or from rain, who can tell.

Many of the cattle ranges in Manatee, Polk and Brevard counties are so much under water and the pasture so drowned out that the cattle are being taken to high ground to save them.

You observe two calamities have befallen Florida this year. First, a freeze out, then a drowned out. A few more such visitations will dampen the ardor of the most sanguine operators. It is said that the Company intend to get machinery to enlarge the canals and make another effort to drain the lakes, with what success is left to a future writer.

It is admitted that the climate of Florida is undergoing a change, that the summers are becoming warmer and wetter; that the winters are colder and severe frosts more frequent; this being the case, there must be and is a cause for it. May it not be that the clearing up of the land, the destruction of the timber and forests and drawing the lakes may have something to do with this state of things, who knows?

We, however do know that God created this world and all things therein, that he looked upon the finished work and pronounced it all very good. But man, God's own creature, is ambitious and must needs attempt to improve on his works. Will or is he able. Nature has certain inexorable laws with penalties attached, and the violation of these laws is sure to bring the penalties. Now God had a wise purpose in all his creations and no doubt Florida with her pine forests, her dense Hammocks sand, lakes and climate, was designed for a special purpose in nature. And now if man by his devices and plans, attempts to change that purpose will he succeed without suffering the penalty, who knows?

USURIOUS EXTORTION.

HOW IT EFFECTS CROPS. THE OPINION OF A FARMER AT GAINESVILLE.

MADISON COUNTY, FLORIDA, August 21; 1886.

AGRICULTURAL EDITOR WEEKLY TIMES:— " I wish you would write up our section in the *Times Union*, in relation to the usurious extortion practiced on our farmers, laborers and poor people generally. For instance one of our farmers will go to a merchant to "run him," that is to help him through; he, the farmer, will have to make a mortgage on his crop, stock, etc., to perhaps twice the amount he wants: say one hundred dollars; from this the money lender takes twenty-five dollars for interest, probably for six months, say from March to October, when the mortgage is due; then sells the farmer forty or fifty dollars worth of goods and charges him the balance of the amount, twenty-five dollars, so the farmer gets fifty dollars worth of supplies for six months, and pays one hundred dollars for them, and if a balance is carried over, he pays interest at the rate of two per cent per month. One honest usurer, an employee of the F. R. and N., charges ten per cent per month.

This whole section, the Black Belt, is eaten up with usury, and the area of Old Field and Broom sedge is rapidly widening in extent.

Some years ago Savannah merchants made advances to farmers, but I have been told that the merchants from interested motives broke these up. When the farmers received aid from Savannah we shipped in 1870 about 3,000 bales of cotton

from Greenville; last year, 1885, we shipped only about 400
bales, a falling off of 2,600 bales. Ancilla can show about the
same record.

Write this up if you please, and can we not get relief? I
am largely interested in land and if the poor people are eaten
up with usury and extortion, of course my land and all the
property of middle Florida will be valueless. We need relief badly, and the whole thing of extortion in middle Florida
ought to be ventilated."   Very truly,

M. W. LINTON.

INTEREST OR USURY ON MONEY LOANED.

All promissory notes, due bills and bank accounts,
draw interest at the rate of eight per cent annum
unless otherwise specified, but any rate, of interest is legal in Florida, when specified in the
writing, note, or contract. Banks charges from
one two three per cent per months on loans, it
depends some on the kind of security and length
of time.

Mortgages on real estate are usually drawn to
draw two per cent per month and sometimes more
than that. The party who gives the mortgages
must pay all expenses of writing, acknowledgeing
recording and releasing, or satisfying the mortgage and very often has to pay a commission to
somebody for negotiating the loan. This makes
the business of borrowing money very expensive.
I know a case where it cost a party something over
twenty dollars to get the use of two hundred dollars for less than forty days.

So long as a man has money of his own in his
pocket, he is all right and can do about as he
pleases, but let him get in debt and have to borrow,

he will then find out the value of money, if not before.

The above was taken from the WEEKLY TIMES of a recent date and while the writer applied the case to middle Florida, it applies equally well to the whole State, and foreshadows what the final result must inevitably be.

THE ORIGIN OF STATE NAMES.

New York—named by the Duke of York, under cover of title given him by the English Crown in 1664.

New Jersey—so-called in honor of Sir George Carteret, who was Governor of the Island of Jersey in the British Channel.

Pennsylvania—from William Penn, the founder of the new colony, meaning Penns woods.

Delaware—in honor of Thomas West Lord de la Ware, who visited the bay and died there in 1610.

Maryland—after Henrietta Maria the Queen of Charles I of England.

Virginia—so-called in honor of Queen Elizabeth, the "virgin Queen," in whose region Sir Walter Raleigh, made the first attempt to colonize that region.

North and South Carolina—were originally in one tract, called Carolina, after Charles IX, of France, in 1601, subsequently in 1665 the name was altered.

Georgia—so-called in honor of George II, of England, who established a colony in that region.

Florida—Ponce de Leon, who discovered that portion of North America in 1519, named it Florida in commemoration of the day he landed there, which was Pasqua de Flores of the Spaniards a feast of flowers, otherwise known as Easter Sunday.

Alabama—formerly a portion of Mississippi Territory, admitted into the Union as a State in 1819. The name is of Indian origin, signifying, "here we rest."

Mississippi—formerly a portion of the Province of Louisi-

ana, so named in 1800 from the great river on the Western line
The term is of Indian origin, meaning the "long river."

Louisiana—from Louis XIV of France, who from some time
prior to 1763, owned the territory.

Arkansas—from Kansas, the Indian name of "Smoky Water"
with the French prefix arc. bow.

Tennesee—Indian name for "the river of the big river," i.e.
the Mississippi, which is the Western boundry.

Kentucky—Indian for "at the head of the river Ohio," from
the Indian meaning beautiful, previously applied to the river
which traverses a great part of its borders.

Michigan—previously applied to the lake, the Indian name
of a fish-wier so-called from the fancied resemblance of the
lake to a fish trap.

Indiana—so-called in 1802 from America Indians.

Illinois—from the Indian "illini" men and the French suf-
fix "ois" together signifying "tribes of men."

Wisconsin—Indian name for wild rushing channel.

Missouri—named in 1820 from the great branch of the Mississippi, which flows through it.

Iowa—Indian named, meaning the drowsy ones.

Minnesota—Indian for cloudy weather.

California—the name given by Cortes, the discoverer of that
region.   He probably obtained it from an old Spanish romance
in which an imaginary island of that name is described as
abounding in gold.

Oregon—according to same from the Oregon river of the
West.   Others say it is derived from the Spanish Oreganoo,
wild Marjourum, which grows on the Pacific coast.

ERRATTA.

PAGE.	LINE.	READ.	FOR.
12	17	about	almost
12	22	foot	feet
12	24	stroke	strike
12	27, 28	bellow	hollow
17	3	through and and	though and are.
19	6	lumber	timber
65	8	item	stem
68	3	stickey	stick
"	14	house	horse
"	16	flower	flour
"	26	are	ore
71	24	clean	clear
83	26	head	neck
95	7	humbuggeries	humbuggers
96	14	taxes	takes
103	15	intended	attended
107	25	say	do
121	25	$1.50	.50
121	28	pound	bushel
121	32, 33	omit	feet
139	27	gloss	glass
151	9	men	man
156	25	help	houses
177	29	vegetation	vegetables
177	42	stockman	stackman
196	13	Greenville	Gainesville

NOTE.

Since writing page 142, nearly all the railroads in Florida have been changed to standard guage.